Reluctant Husband

SPECIAL EDITION

WHISKEY MEN
BOOK ONE

HOPE FORD

For my Mom, always. I would never have written one book if it wasn't for you. I love you.

For all my Instalove friends. Thank you.
Your friendship means the world to me.
Thank you for encouraging me when I said I wanted to write this book. XX

CHAPTER 1

Isabella

I'm scanning the front page of the newspaper as I walk up the steps to Lottie's room. She may be eighty-one years old, but if there's any mention of her five grandsons, she'll spot it quickly, and heads are going to roll. She likes them to stay out of the gossip column, but it seems one, two, or heck, all five of them make their way into it at some point or another, and I'm just trying to save their asses and keep their grandmother from getting upset at the same time.

I almost trip on the stairs when I turn the paper upside down and spot Lucas Blaze. I should have known one of them would make the front page, even if it is the bottom. And there he is. Lucas Blaze, youngest brother of the billion-dollar whiskey company. He's got his arm around some woman, and even though it looks innocent enough, the headline reads *Lucas Blaze is on the Prowl Again*. I would laugh at the stupid headline, but I'm too busy staring at the man in question. He looks good, but he always looks good. And just like every other time I see him, there's a tightness in my chest and a flutter in my belly. Forcing my eyes off him, I fold up the paper as I get to the open doors of Lottie's bedroom and en suite living room. There's no way I can take this paper in there. No way! Heck, I don't want to see the disappointment on her face, and I definitely don't want to get into a conversation about Lucas and how he needs to settle down. I mean, yeah, I wish it would happen, but I can't see it happening anytime soon and definitely not with the likes of me.

I stow it on the hall table, force a smile onto my face, and walk in. My smile falters just a little when I spot Lottie sitting in her chair with a pale face. If nothing else, the woman always has her makeup on. She says you can't face the day if you're not ready, and to her, ready is dressed, made up, and hair done, and she wouldn't be caught dead without earrings.

She must see the worried look on my face because she points at the table next to her with all her makeup strewn about. "I'm getting to it. I just needed a little rest."

I sit on the chair in front of her and shrug. "I think you're beautiful without it."

She reaches for me, and her frail hand squeezes mine. Her strength may not be what it used to be, but the sentiment is the same. "You're too good to me, Issi."

I smile and shake my head. "I could say the same about you." The fact is, I could say a lot more. Lottie was my grandmother's best friend and like a second grandmother to me growing up. Especially when my own grandma passed away. I know she's trying to fill the huge gap in my life since she passed, and I love her for it. We've always been close but even more so lately. "What do you think, G?" I call her by the nickname I gave her a long time ago. "Do you want to go naked today?"

She gasps, and a look of shock lights up her face. "Naked! Well, I never, Isabelle Stevens."

I can feel my face flush hot. "I meant your face... no makeup."

She bursts out laughing. "I knew what you meant. I'm just giving you a hard time. I want to at least put some mascara on. I can't let people think I'm already dead."

She lifts the tube of mascara, and her hands shake as she tries to unscrew it. It's hard seeing her like this, but there's no way I would walk away from her. "Let me do it, G."

She hands over the tube easily, and I take it from her. "So did you sleep well?"

And as soon as I say it, I know it was the wrong thing to say. I'm sure she remembers that last night was the big fundraiser in Jasper and that the Jasper newspaper worked through the night to get the papers delivered this morning. Her eyes widen, even as I'm coming at her with the wand in my hand. "Where's the paper?" she asks.

I should have thought this through a little bit because there's no way to avoid her gaze while applying mascara to her lashes. "Hold still."

She opens her eyes wider and holds still. I finish one eye, and she doesn't hesitate. "Okay, so what happened last night? Have you heard from any of my grandsons? What about Lucas? Is he up this morning yet?"

"Hold still," I tell her again and lean in for the other eye. She does as I ask, but I know this is not something she's going to let go. I finish the second eye, screw the cap, and grab the handheld mirror on the table. "What do you think?"

She barely glances at the mirror. "Yeah, yeah, Issi. It's great, thank you. So where's the paper?"

I wince even though I'm trying hard to keep my reactions hidden. "I think it's in the hallway."

She rears back, confusion on her face. "Why would it be... shitfire... they're in there. They've done something, haven't they? Those five grandsons of mine are going to be the death of me yet."

"Now, G. There's no reason to get upset. No one did anything scandalous or anything." Damn, I hope they didn't anyway. I really don't want to be lying to her right now.

She holds her hand out to me. "Bring me the paper." And as an afterthought, she adds, "Please."

I stand up from my chair to go get the paper. When I come back in, I hold it out to her, and she takes it. I have to give her credit. She may be getting up in age, and her eyesight might not be what it used to be, but she finds the column a lot faster than I did. She scans the article and then zones in on the picture of Lucas before dropping the paper in her lap. "First of all, it says five most eligible bachelors. Only four of my grandsons are eligible. How is it that they always forget Beau is married and has been for some time now? How do they think Natalie feels about that?"

I know Lottie doesn't expect an answer, so I keep my mouth shut. But I know she's right. I really like Natalie, and the last few times I've seen her, there has been a sadness in her eyes. I can't help but wonder if everything is okay with her and Beau. Before I can get too lost in thought, Lottie picks up the paper again and points at the picture, reading the caption. *"On the prowl."* She flicks her hand at the paper in frustration. "That boy needs to settle down, and that's all there is to it."

I'm not going to call it panic, but there's a part of me that feels the urgency of her words. "He's the youngest brother, G. Don't you think you should start on the others first?"

I scrunch my nose up as soon as the words leave my mouth. I always tell myself to stay out of it when she gets like this, but it looks like I can't keep my mouth shut when it comes to Lucas. The fact is, I hate seeing pictures of him with other women. It guts me in a way that I've never felt before, but what Lottie is wanting seems too much to me. How in the world can I be here when he's in love with another woman? Can I stay on, working as Lottie's nurse and taking care of her while crossing paths with Lucas' serious girlfriend or even wife in the hallway? I don't think my heart can handle it.

Lottie reaches for me, holding on to both of my hands. "They all need to find a good woman and get married. And Beau... don't get me started on him. He needs to fix whatever he's got going on with Natalie. But Lucas... He needs, hell more than any of them, he needs to find a woman that will love him like he deserves to be loved. He doesn't trust anyone... He thinks they'll all leave and how.... How can I leave here not knowing that someone is here for him, Issi?"

I know that Lucas and Lottie are close. I may not know the whole story, but I remember my own grandmother saying that Lottie was like a mother to him. Plus, the fact remains that while all the other brothers have their own homes, Lucas lives in his grandmother's home. It's not because he can't afford one of his own, that's for sure. No, he chooses to stay here. I take in a deep breath and let it out slowly. "First of all, you know I hate it when you talk about leaving us. I don't want to even think about it. Second of all, Lucas is a very capable man. Yeah, he works too much, but he's happy."

"Happy!" she harumphs. "He wouldn't know happy if it bit him in the ass."

I try to contain my laughter because it always cracks me up when G throws in curse words. She's all regal, classy and conservative, but I think she uses them to throw us all off. "Okay, so talk to him. Let him know you're worried about him. You know that man better than any of us, but even I know he'd give you anything you asked for. He loves you, Lottie. We all do."

She nods her head. "I know. I just...."

I cut her off and squeeze her hands. "I know. You need to know when you leave that your family is going to be okay. I get that. I really do." I bite my lower lip and try not to think about Lucas settling down. I wasn't lying. If Lottie asked him to, he'd do it in a heartbeat. I'll just have to deal with whatever happens because even though I love Lucas, I know he would never notice me.

"All right, so you've stalled long enough. I think it's time we got up to do our morning exercise. What do you think?"

CHAPTER 2

Lucas

I stand outside the doors of my grandmother's wing of the house. I've stood here for way too long eavesdropping. Fuck! I want to scream it from the rooftops, but I know doing so is not going to give me any kind of peace. I hate hearing my grandmother talk this way. Fuck, any time she talks about leaving, it literally makes me nauseous. She's been like a mother to me my whole life. A real mom... not like the woman that gave birth to me.

The sound of rap music draws me out of my musings as a man sings about getting tipsy in the club. Instantly a smile forms on my lips. My grandmother hates exercise, any and every form of it, but what gets her moving is rap music. I don't get it, and I've long since given up trying to explain it. It brings me back to when I was younger and she used to make me dance with her to this music. Country music is more my speed, but for Grandma, I'd do anything. I lean against the doorjamb and peer inside.

Sure enough, Granny and Isabella are standing up dancing. Well, Granny is more just softly swaying back and forth, but I smile watching my grandmother. She always seems to get lost in the music, and she's obviously happy. I let my gaze trail over to Isabella. Her long brown hair is in a ponytail, and it's swinging back and forth as she moves to the music. She's clapping along with my grandmother, and the way they're smiling at each other, it's obvious how much they love and care about each other.

My grandma stops and hollers over the music, "Here comes the chorus, Issi. Do it!"

Isabella is already shaking her head side to side. "No..."

Granny claps her hands together. "Do it, Issi. Please... for me."

And when the chorus comes on, Isabella breaks into some kind of dance routine. It seems I'm not the only one that will give Granny what she wants.

I should look away. I know I should announce that I'm here, but as I watch Issi grind her hips, shake side to side, pop to a squat and back again, all while gyrating her hips, there's nothing I can do but stare with my mouth hanging open. Isabella is the timid girl that used to hang out with our grandmas. When she wasn't with them, she always had her nose stuck in a book. We rarely crossed paths a lot, and when we did, not much was said. We are from two different worlds, and even though I've always tried to be nice to her, that's as far as it's ever gone.

But standing here, watching her move her hips, it seems there's a side to Isabella that I've never seen before. I shift my stance as I watch her thick hips shimmy side to side. I can feel my attraction growing, and if I don't do something about it, it's going to be obvious to everyone what I'm standing here thinking about.

I clear my throat, but no one notices. I do it again, louder this time.

Both women stop and stare at me. Granny just smiles, but Isabella's face turns at least ten shades of red before she walks over to the speaker and turns it down. "We were... we were just getting our exercise in."

I put my hands on my hips. "And what? You thought dancing was the right exercise for her? And to rap music, no less."

I regret it as soon as I say it. I don't know what it is, but it seems that lately, Isabella brings out the worst in me. I should probably try to figure that out, but there's something holding me back from doing it.

Isabella, who's never one time stood up to me, brings her arms up to cross on her chest. "Actually, any movement is good for her, and dancing is something that brings her joy."

I cross my arms over my chest, mirroring her. "And the rap music?"

She opens her mouth and then closes it again. Finally, she blurts. "What? I like rap music. There's nothing wrong with it."

My lips twitch, but I refuse to give in to the smile. So Isabella is not going to call my grandmother out for her surprising taste in music. Before I can come up with a response, Isabella is making her way to the door. "I'm going to go check on your breakfast, G. I'll be back."

I watch as she walks out the door. Her jeans are tight across her ass, and I resist the urge to reach out and stop her.

"She's something... isn't she?"

My grandma's words draw my eyes from the door, and I look at her with a closed expression. "Actually, I was thinking that maybe we should hire a nurse with more experience."

"No!" Granny says without any qualms whatsoever. She points her finger at me. "So help me Lucas, if you try to bring another nurse in here, I'll run them off. All of them. I want Issi."

I hold my hands up in defeat. "Fine, whatever you say, Granny. I just want what's best for you. You know that."

She walks toward her chair and sits down with a big sigh. I see the paper on the table, and she grabs it, holding it up to me. "Do you want to talk about this?"

I shake my head and sit down on the chair in front of her. "No," I answer honestly. "But I have a feeling that doesn't matter."

She holds it toward me, pointing at the picture of me at last night's fundraiser. I'm dancing with the daughter of one of the biggest donors. It was all innocent. It wasn't like I brought her home or anything.

"I thought I asked you guys to stay out of the paper. Blaze Whiskey doesn't need any negative exposure."

I grab the paper and scan it. "It was a fundraiser. You know they're going to take a picture, Granny. And we're just dancing."

She points at the paper. "Read the caption."

Lucas Blaze is on the Prowl Again.

It goes on, but I'm not interested in anything it has to say. "I can't help what they write about us. I mean, look. They obviously don't know. It says five most eligible bachelors. They have to know Beau is married."

I'm probably going to hell for it, but yes, I'm trying to get Granny off the topic of me and my love life and instead on one of my brothers.

She shakes her head. "Don't get me started. I'm going to be making a call to the paper later today about that, but what I want to talk about now is you."

I feign innocence like I don't know exactly where this conversation is going. "Me? What about me?"

She groans in frustration, and I stand up, pulling my phone from my pocket. I turn on the Bluetooth and connect to the speaker system. A soft slow song fills the air, and I pocket my phone and hold my hand out to her. "Dance with me, Granny."

She doesn't hesitate in getting up, but as soon as she puts her hand in mine, she starts again. "This is nice, Lucas, but your charm is not going to get you out of it today. I want to talk to you."

I slowly twirl her around, holding on to her the whole time. Our movements are slow and a little clunky, but I don't care. She loves to dance, and I feel like the longer she keeps doing it, the longer she'll be here. "Fine. Talk to me. I'm listening."

She pats me on the chest. She's panting a little, and

I slow us down, only swaying back and forth. I'm holding her up, but she's pretty frail these days, so it's like holding nothing.

She looks up at me. I take in the small lines around her eyes, and even though she's still beautiful, she seems to have aged just in the last few weeks alone. "But are you listening? Really, Lucas? Because I need you to hear what I'm saying."

I nod, not taking my eyes off hers. "I'm listening, Granny."

She pats me on the chest and leans into me. "You have to be open to love, Lucas. And when you find it, you have to hold on to it."

I could have quoted her word for word, but I kept quiet. Granny has said that exact sentence to me over and over my whole life. When I was younger, it was just something she said. But as I grew up, I started to think about it. Really think about it. And I know she's right. I do. But there's always a part of me that wonders if I'm worthy of love and a bigger part of me that knows that women leave. Why would I want to put myself through that? But I swallow down everything I want to say and tell her what she wants to hear. "I know you're right, Granny. I'm working on it."

Her eyes widen in surprise. "You are?"

I nod, looking her straight in the eye. I've never

been able to lie to my grandmother before, but hearing her talk to Isabella earlier and knowing how concerned she is for me, I'd do anything–even lie–to make her feel better. "Yeah, I think it's time I start working on me. I want to have kids one day–"

She cuts me off. "You do?"

I laugh. "Of course I do, Granny."

Her hands tighten on my shirt. "What about Issi?"

I stop swaying and then start again. "Uh, what about her?"

Granny looks up at me with so much hope on her face. "I always thought you and she would be perfect together. It's obvious she loves you. Have you thought about asking her out on a date? Maybe get to know her better?"

I try to keep the guard up on my face as my stomach does a little somersault. What does she mean Issi loves me? The woman acts as if she can barely tolerate me. If I come into a room, she leaves as fast as she can. She never talks to me except to give me yes or no answers. Heck, today was the first time she's said more than just a sentence or two at a time to me. There's no way she loves me. "Now, Granny... " I start, wanting to appease her.

She's not having it, though. She stops and shakes her head. "Look, Lucas, would I love to see you and

Isabella together? Absolutely. Would I love to see you happy–"

I start to interrupt her and tell her that I am indeed happy, but she swats me on the chest, stopping me. "No, I mean truly happy, and don't even try to lie to me and say you are happy. Are you content with your life? Sure. But I want you to have it all, Lucas. You deserve to be loved... You just have to be open to it."

I start to nod, but Granny's not done yet. "And look, I'm worried about what will happen to Issi when I go. You have your brothers; she has no one."

All I can do is stare back at the woman that has loved me unconditionally my last thirty-four years. Speechless, I know what she's asking of me. I know what she wants, but I can't promise her that yet. Fuck, I want to give her everything she wants, and it's on the very tip of my tongue to do just that, but instead, I murmur, "I promise you, Granny. I will make sure she's okay."

She tilts her head and looks at me as if she's trying to weigh my words, and by the pinched look on her face, she's finding them underwhelming. "And I'll get to know her... spend some time with her."

Granny turns and grabs on to the arm of her chair before settling into it. "Thank you, Lucas. Thank you so much. You won't regret it. All I'm saying is to be open to it. Imagine if you and Isabella ended up getting married. Oh, Lucas, you've made this old woman happy."

I plop down in the chair across from her. I know in her head, she's already planning a wedding, but I don't have the heart to stop her. Surely, there's another way.

CHAPTER 3

Isabella

"So what did Lottie say?" Bridget asks me.

I'm huffing and puffing, mostly from holding my breath as I quietly ran away from Lottie's door and then down the stairs. I try to pull myself together. "Oatmeal. She said oatmeal was fine."

Bridget looks at me strangely. "Are you okay?"

I nod and start to ramble. "Great. I'm good. Just fine."

She shakes her head and turns back to the stove, mumbling something about kids these days. I'm twenty-five years old, but to Bridget, I'm a child. She says it enough. She's worked for the family for as long as I can remember, and even though she's gruff most of the time, she really is a good person. "Thanks, Bridget."

She shrugs and goes about setting the tray. At the request of Bridget, I went upstairs to see if Lottie wanted oatmeal or some peanut butter toast this morning, but when I got upstairs, there was a slow country tune on the speakers, and Lucas was dancing with his grandmother. Instantly, I'd pulled my phone from my pocket and started recording. He was mostly holding her up–our dancing earlier obviously wore her out–but even so, there was love shining on her face as she looked up at Lucas. I hadn't planned to eavesdrop. It was innocent enough. I was wanting to catch a sweet moment between the two of them. I had no idea what I would overhear by standing there.

I definitely didn't expect G to tell Lucas that I was in love with him. I put my hand over my heart and lean on the counter. I feel a pressure in my chest, and I can't seem to catch my breath. I want to run. Heck, run as fast and as far as I can. I can just imagine what Lucas is thinking. He's going to fire me. I'm pretty sure he's been looking for a reason to get rid of me, which is why I've been living out of my suitcase here for the last three months.

I don't know which one causes me more grief: the fact I'm probably fired and won't be able to see G anymore, or the fact that Lucas now knows how I feel about him.

"I'm taking this to Lottie."

I nod and force a smile to my face as Bridget walks from the kitchen carrying the tray in her hands. As soon as she's gone, I lean my head down on the cool countertop and groan. This whole situation is not ideal. I could have gone my whole life without Lucas knowing how I felt about him, but I can't be mad at Lottie. I know her heart is in the right place even if it is a little bit misguided. I turn my head to the side and press my cheek to the cool tile. I feel hot all over, and I'm about to walk over and stick my head in the refrigerator when I hear Lucas ask, "Are you okay?"

I freeze, my back to him, and then I bolt up, realizing that I'm leaning over his kitchen counter, and all he can see is my large ass up in the air. Fuck, what is wrong with me? I grab a towel that's setting off to the side and start wiping down the counter I was just leaning over. Cleaning is not any part of my job, but I need to be busy. "Yes, fine. I'm good. You off to work?" I grimace. "I mean, it's none of my business. You don't have to answer that. Have a nice day. Be careful."

I completely blurt it all out in one big breath, and then I force my mouth closed to keep from rambling and making an even bigger fool of myself.

I still haven't looked at him, but I can feel him move closer to me. *Breathe, Isabella. Breathe,* I tell myself.

I suck in a deep breath and let it out slowly.

He comes to stand in front of me and is watching me. I cover my arms over my chest and figure the best offense is a good defense. "Dancing is how she exercises. She doesn't like walking or Pilates; all the ups and downs is too hard for her. I promise I've tried it all, and dancing is what makes her happy."

I seem to have surprised him. He opens his mouth and closes it. I look him straight in the eye because I know if I don't, I'll be looking at the way his button-down shirt stretches across his chest. Or the way the sleeves are fitted against his muscular arms. Not that looking at his face is helping me any. Lucas is a very handsome man with his dark hair and eyes. His hair is getting a little long and hanging on his forehead. I form my hand into a fist to stop myself from reaching for him and pushing it off his face.

He tilts his head to the side. "And the music? You think rap music is the most appropriate for her to be dancing to? I mean, not that I didn't enjoy your little twerking–"

My mouth falls open. "I wasn't twerking."

He shrugs. "Trust me, honey, it sure looked like twerking."

I put my face in my hands, embarrassed, and then it hits me. Did he just say he enjoyed it? My head snaps up, and my eyes fly to his. He's looking at me in a way he's never looked at me before, but of course it could just be that he thinks I'm going to throw myself at him any minute. What I thought was a lifting of his lips drops, and he stares back at me, guarded.

I put my hands on my hips. "Look, I know you don't like me. I know you don't think I'm the best person for this job."

He shakes his head slowly. "I didn't say that."

I take a step toward him, and he takes a step back. My hands fist at my sides. Yep, he thinks I'm going to throw myself at him. I stand perfectly still, not leaning toward him like my body wants to. "You don't have to say it. It's obvious, and that's fine. But I promise you that there's nothing I wouldn't do for your grandmother. I love her, and if there is any point where I feel that I'm not qualified to take care of her, you will be the first to know. I promise." As an afterthought, I add, "And I never break a promise."

I say it with all sincerity because it's the truth. I do love his grandmother, and I'd do anything for her.

He doesn't say anything. I figured he'd give me

some kind of warning, something, but all he does is stand in front of me and stare at me. The silence becomes a little overwhelming, especially when he looks me up and down. I'm not prepared as his gaze travels down my body and up again. My nipples are puckered tight, and I cross my arms over my chest to hide the arousal I feel from him looking at me. Heck, just a look and I'm like a cat in heat, ready and willing to slide my body along his.

His nostrils flare, but that's the only change to his face. "I know you love Lottie."

I wait for more, but nothing else comes. I point up toward the ceiling. "I'd better get back up there."

I turn to leave, but he reaches out, grabbing my arm to stop me. "Do you have a boyfriend, Isabella?"

I clench my eyes. Well, damn. He's probably worried about me living in his house now. He probably thinks that I'm going to be throwing myself at him or damn, sneaking into his bedroom. Without turning around, I answer him. "I don't think that's any of your business, Lucas."

I tug on my arm, but he doesn't let go. If anything, he steps toward me, and I can feel the warmth of his body along my outstretched arm. "Look at me," he demands.

I turn my head and lift my eyes to his but remain silent.

His grip tightens, but it doesn't hurt. I'm too surprised by the look in his eye. "I don't want any strange men here."

I shake my head, not understanding. "Strange men?"

He grits his teeth. "Any men. You're here to do a job."

Oh God, I have no clue what he's thinking. Wait, he's obviously not thinking. "The only friend over is Carlotta, and your grandmother loves to have her visit."

He lets out a breath and finally releases me. "Okay."

Okay? That's it? What is even happening here? Is he afraid I'm going to bring someone in to steal the family's whiskey recipe secrets or what? I search his eyes, trying to read what he's thinking, but now he's looking back at me with a guarded look on his face. "I would never bring anyone questionable around G... or any of you, for that matter."

He shakes his head. "It's not that... forget it. Forget I said anything. Thank you for taking care of my grandmother and for playing along when she insists on dancing to that music."

My mouth falls open. "You knew?"

He's still holding on to my arm, and his thumb is running in circles around my wrist. "Did I know that my grandmother's favorite music was rap? Yes, I did. I've danced to it with her way more times than I care to admit."

I smile at him as he smiles at me. For once, it feels like we're on the same side and sharing a secret together. It would be so easy to lean into him and ask him to tell me more, but I refuse to embarrass myself more than I already have today. I gently pull my arm from his hold. "Have a good day at work."

Before he can answer, I'm walking out of the kitchen and putting much-needed distance between Lucas and me. It's something I need to do before my mind starts going crazy and thinking that maybe, just maybe, there could be something between Lucas Blaze and me.

CHAPTER 4

Lucas

I can't get this morning out of my head. As soon as I get to the office, my day turns crazy. I have appointments, meetings, phone calls, emails to answer, and the list goes on. But the whole day, thoughts of Isabella are in the back of my mind.

At the end of the day, I have a meeting scheduled with my brothers. We do this every week, and it's just a time to get caught up. Ford, as the CEO, gets us started and talks about the big picture, as he likes to call it. Beau comes in next with a bunch of numbers, and I always try my best to not fall asleep as he goes over diagrams and spreadsheets. Austin's turn is always the most fun. He talks about how the distillery is doing, what's working and what's not, but he always has stories about some mishap or gossip with the employees. Then it's my turn, and I talk about how I'm expanding the brand into new markets and where I'm at with whatever companies I'm talking to. We always get the business out of the way first, and today isn't any different.

As soon as I finish my spiel, Beau asks the rest of us, "Anyone heard from Huddy?"

Hudson is our brother, but instead of joining the family business, he went into the military. He's served for twenty years, and the talk recently is that he's going to be retiring soon, and we need to make a position for him with the company. "No, I haven't," I answer.

The rest of the guys chime in with the same answer.

"He's not going to want to wear a suit and tie. You know that, right?" Austin chimes in.

Ford, the oldest, always takes charge of any situation, and he shrugs his shoulders. "He doesn't have to, but it's going to be hard for him getting out, and we need to have a place for him if he does want it. The choice is his, though."

We talk about a few other things, and after Ford ends the meeting, everyone gets up to leave. I stop Beau as he's piling his charts and papers together. "Hey, heads up. Granny saw in the paper the quote about us being the five most eligible bachelors. Is there a reason people don't know you're married?"

He grits his teeth but doesn't look at me. "They know I'm married, for fuck's sake. I don't know what their problem is."

"Well, Granny is taking care of it. She's calling the paper today, so I'm sure heads are going to roll."

Finally, Beau lifts his head. "How is Granny?"

I shrug. They all just saw her at the last Sunday dinner. "Same."

He gives me one nod before putting his notebook under his arm and telling us goodbye.

I get up to leave, and Ford points at the chair I was sitting in. Austin makes some kind of face at me, like I'm in trouble or something, and I flip him off as he walks out of the conference room. I don't sit, though. I stand next to the chair I just vacated. "What is it, Ford?"

He leans forward. "What's going on with you? Are you okay?"

I'm not ready to share what I've been thinking, so I tap my pen on the desk. "What do you mean what's going on with me? I'm good. I'm fine."

He doesn't believe me. I can tell by the way he tilts his head with that smirk on his face. "You were zoned out during the whole meeting."

"Beau—" I start, but he doesn't let me finish.

"No, I'm used to you—hell, we all zone out during Beau's presentations of charts and diagrams. But even Austin's story about the guy that singed all his arm hair off didn't make you laugh."

I rear back, wide-eyed. "A guy caught his arm hair on fire?"

Ford points at me. "See! That right there. You were zoned out. What's going on? Talk to me. Is Granny worse?"

I might as well give it up. I'm not getting out of here until I tell him. "No, Granny's fine. I mean, no change. She still gets tired easy. Even dancing—the only form of exercise she's willing to do—she just sways back and forth now. I literally have to hold her up. But there's been no change since Sunday."

Ford stands up and leans against the table, arms over his chest. He's giving me that big brother look—the one where I'm not getting out of here until I tell him. "So I had a conversation with Granny this morning, and she gave me a few things to think about."

He tenses. "Oh yeah? What's that?"

I tell him about overhearing Granny and Isabella this morning, leaving out the part where she said she thinks Isabella loves me. And then I tell him about my talk with Granny. "She wants me to settle down. She's worried about me, and she's worried about Isabella when"–I try not to choke up–"when Granny leaves us."

Ford stands to his full height and comes toward me. His hand goes to my shoulder and squeezes. "She's not the only one that's worried about you, Lucas."

Our eyes meet, and I see the worry in his. He's the oldest brother. He was ten years old when I was born, but he may as well have been twenty. He looked after us, and to this day, we all look up to him. "It's going to be hard for all of us," I say.

He nods but lifts his shoulders in a shrug. "I know that. We'll all grieve. Granny is one of a kind, and we'll all miss her. But your relationship with her is different than the rest of us. If anything, she's been like a mother to you."

I know what he's saying. When our mother left, Granny stepped in for all of us. My dad remarried a few years later, and Charlotte is great, but I had attached myself to Granny by then. She really has been like a mother to me. "Yeah, uh, she's also worried about Isabella."

Ford's forehead creases, and before I can change my mind, I spit it out. "Granny has it in her head that Isabella and I should be together. I think–no, I know– she wants us to get married."

His mouth compresses into a hard line, and he shakes his head. "Don't do it, Lucas. Don't even think about it."

Surprised that he obviously feels this strongly about it, I lift my shoulders in a shrug. "Why not? We can get married and give Granny some peace. You should have heard her, man. She really wants this."

Ford leans onto the table, pressing his fist into the hard cherry wood. "You can't marry her."

I cross my arms over my chest. The days where Ford tells me what to do and I do it without question passed around the time I hit puberty. And even though I fully respect him, this isn't something I'm going to let him sway me on. But I am curious. "Why? You seem to feel awfully strong about this. What? You like Isabella or something?"

I try to act like I don't care one way or another, but already my hands are fisting at my sides. All in one day, this woman has me turned inside out. I'm not a jealous person. At least I didn't think I was.

Ford throws his hand in the air. "Of course not. But you can't lead her on like that. She obviously loves you, and when it ends, you're going to break her heart. And even though I think Granny should have everything she wants, Issi doesn't deserve to be a casualty in all this."

The way Ford shortens her name sends me into a silent panic. What the fuck? I didn't even think he knew Isabella except in casual crossing. And what the hell does he mean, she loves me? "That's twice today that I've been told Isabella loves me. She does not love me."

Ford presses his hands to his eyes and rubs them before giving me a look of complete exasperation. "Oh my God, Lucas. You're blind. So blind. The woman is crazy for you. You walk into a room and she can't take her eyes off you. I'm telling you if you do this, you're going to hurt her, and she doesn't deserve that. She's going to grieve too, Lucas, and we'll all be there for her, but we don't need to add a broken heart to the things she's going to have to deal with."

I'm stubborn. Probably too stubborn for my own good. "Well, I guess it's a good thing that I'm a grown man now and can make my own decisions."

Ford opens his mouth, but I cut him off. "What about Ollie's soccer game? It's starting soon, right?"

Ford looks at the clock on the wall. "Fuck!"

He grabs his papers off the desk and is headed for the door. "Way to end the conversation, brother, but I'm telling you, Granny wants you happy and settled, but she wouldn't want the poor girl's heart broken."

I hold my hands up in front of me. "I promise you. I will not hurt Isabella."

He gives me the look like he doesn't believe a fuckin' word I just said, but we both know he doesn't have time to argue with me about it. "I'll see you at the game."

He walks out the door, and I close up the conference room with all my thoughts on Isabella.

CHAPTER 5

Isabella

I've tried to hide my worry from G, and I think I've been successful, but I'm worn out from the façade. Lucas came home late last night, and by the way he slammed the door to his wing of the house, I assumed he wasn't happy. And then this morning, when he left without even coming in to see his grandmother, I knew something was up. As a matter of fact, that was probably the kicker. He's never missed a morning of coming in and talking to his grandmother. Not since I've been here. But instead of letting G worry with me, I made up an excuse of an early meeting as to why he didn't come see her this morning.

She smiled and didn't seem worried, but I still tried to keep her busy all day. As the late afternoon comes, and Ford shows up with his son Ollie, I'm able to relax a little. Surely, if something was wrong with Lucas, Ford wouldn't be here all smiles.

Ollie is sitting in the chair next to his great-grandmother, telling her about his game from the night before. "I scored a goal, Granny!"

She claps her hand excitedly. "I know you did. I'm so proud of you. I've watched the video at least twenty times today."

I sit in the corner of the room to give the family time to spend together. Usually I make myself scarce, but the night shift nurse should be arriving soon, and I want to make sure I tell her that G has already eaten and taken her afternoon medications.

I'm taking pictures with my phone of Ollie, Ford, and G all together when Ford says, "So are you still listening to rap music, Granny?"

G looks at me like I've sold her out. I hold my hands up and give her my most innocent look. "Don't look at me. You know I wouldn't tell on you. I haven't said a word."

Granny is all smiles, enjoying the teasing. "I'll have you know, grandson, that I have impeccable taste in music. Ask anyone."

Ford stands up and pulls his phone from his pocket. He scrolls on it, and when a song starts to play, he points at his Grandma. "No, Granny, this is good music."

A slow country ballad comes over the speakers, and Granny points between Ford and me. "Go ahead. Show us how it's done."

Ollie goes to sit next to G, and Ford walks over to me with his hand held out. I stand up and meet him at the center of the room. I wish I could be this way with Lucas. Instead I'm all tongue-tied and worried I'm going to say or do something stupid. With Ford, I guess I don't care, so I don't try to hide anything. He's good on his feet, and he twirls me around the room. Ollie and G are both laughing and clapping. Ford is really showing off, spinning me around and pulling me back in. I can't help but laugh when I miss a step and almost face-plant. Ford saves me easily, though, and pulls me up again to twirl some more.

Ollie comes to stand next to us. "I want to dance, Daddy."

I let go of Ford, but he shakes his head. "Oh no, you're not getting out of it that easily."

He puts Ollie, himself, and me in a little circle, and we all dance together. Ollie's laughter is infectious, and we're all laughing and having a good time. We're completely ignoring the speed of the music, dancing too fast for the slow beat, but none of us seem to care.

I look over at G smiling at all of us, and I can't help but point out to her, "Well, you've succeeded in getting out of your exercise, I see."

G's eyes twinkle at me.

Ollie releases his hold on his dad and me and runs to his great-grandmother. "I'll dance with you, Granny."

She grabs on to his hand, and he dances in front of her while she sits, tapping her feet back and forth. It's obvious she's worn out today.

With Ollie and G occupied, Ford pulls me back into his arms. I grin up at him, taking in his smiling face with the gray-streaked beard. He really is a handsome guy. All the Blaze brothers are. He looks at his grandmother and back at me. "She doing okay?"

I nod. "Yes, but she's getting tired more easily. We'll probably have to cut back on the dancing."

He nods and looks at me curiously. "What about you? You holding up okay?"

I force a smile to my face. "Yes, I'm great. I got this, Ford. I promise I will take the best care of your grand–"

He cuts me off. "I wasn't asking because I thought you weren't qualified. I was asking because I know how you feel about her. I know it's hard for you to see her deteriorate like this. It's hard on all of us, but we get a break from it. You don't. I'm just worried about you, that's all."

I tuck my chin onto his shoulder because I can't look into his eyes. I know it's his granny, and I should be the one comforting him, but honestly, I don't know what I'll do when she leaves us. It's not something I want to even think about.

Ford pulls back and looks into my face. "Hey."

I reluctantly lift my head to look him in the eyes. "I know. I appreciate it. We'll get through it. We just need to enjoy every second we have left."

A small smile slowly forms on his face. "You're right. You're absolutely right."

I nod and let him twirl me out and back in. "So do I need to talk to you about my little brother?"

I groan and lean my forehead against his chest. Gee whiz. First Granny and now Ford. "Let's not talk about him."

"You know that when we asked you to do this, we had no idea how you felt about Lucas?"

I want to bang my head against something. "Does everyone in this family know how I feel about Lucas? It's reaching a point where it's embarrassing."

He shakes his head. "Embarrassing? It shouldn't be embarrassing for you at all. If Lucas was any other man, he'd be thanking his lucky stars right now and trying to figure out how to keep you."

I don't miss the meaning. "If he was any other man? Meaning that since he's Lucas..."

He sighs. "Meaning that of all of us, Lucas probably has the most scars from our mom leaving us. She literally walked away the day he was born. Left him in the hospital while my dad went to get a cup of coffee."

I gasp as I feel tears forming in my eyes. "Oh my God. I had no idea."

He nods. "Yeah, so see, don't take it personally. I don't know if Lucas will ever get his head out of his ass and believe in love and forever. I mean, he doesn't have the best examples to look up to."

I know he's talking about himself and his own failed divorce too. It still blows my mind that the woman walked away from Ford and Ollie. Who leaves their own son? I guess Ollie and Lucas are a lot alike in that regard, and no doubt he's worried about how all this is going to affect Ollie when he grows up.

Lost in thought, Ford nudges me. "So I guess what I'm saying is, don't get your heart broken. My brother is one of the best... but he can't give you what you want."

I nod and squeeze his shoulder. "So this is what this is like, huh?"

His forehead creases. "What what's like?"

I try to hide my smile, but I swat him in the chest. "Having a big brother that butts into your business. Man, I'm starting to appreciate this whole only child thing."

He laughs a big, deep belly laugh, and thankfully, his smile returns. We continue dancing as Ollie and G are in deep conversation. But even as I sway back and forth in Ford's arms, all I can think about is Lucas. I never knew the full story about his mother, and now that I do, I see him in a different light. I know Ford was trying to warn me against falling for him, but all he's succeeded in doing is giving me a new understanding of why he is the way he is. I know it's farfetched, but if I ever have a chance with Lucas, I'll take it. And I'll hold on to it for dear life.

CHAPTER 6

Lucas

I t's been a day.

I knew rushing out this morning was a mistake, and I felt guilty about it all day. I can't remember the last time that I left without telling my grandmother goodbye. Hell, I don't think I ever have. But it's not just that. I was off all day, and I think I finally figured it out around mid-afternoon. I had missed talking to Isabella this morning. Yeah, it's usually one-sided, and I usually give her some shit about something, but that's become our thing... and I missed it.

I didn't want to examine it or try to figure out what I'm thinking. Instead, I cut out of work early to head home. As soon as I open the front door, I hear the laughing. Ollie, my nephew, must be here because I can hear his expressive voice all the way down the steps. I throw my briefcase onto the entryway table and take my suit jacket off, hanging it on a hook before taking the steps two at a time.

The closer I get to Granny's door, the faster my heart starts to race. I'm about to walk in when I stop at the sight in front of me. Granny and Ollie are sitting off to the side, deep in conversation. But that's not what has my heart stopping, my hands fisting, and my eyes widening. No, it's the sight of my older brother dancing with his arms around Isabella. I stay rooted to my spot and can't take my eyes off them.

It's hard seeing them together and Isabella tucked against his chest. They seem to be having a discussion, and I watch them closely, wondering if the reason Ford warned me off yesterday was because he does in fact have a thing for Isabella.

I'm so lost in thought that I barely register it when Ollie hollers and bounds toward me. "Uncle Lucas!"

I have just enough time to brace myself as he jumps into my arms. I hold him up and walk with him back over to Granny. "What's up, little dude?"

He huffs. "Little? I'm not little. I'm in kindergarten."

I laugh because how could I not? Especially with him smiling up at me and his two front teeth missing. "Oh wow! Kindergarten. How could I forget?" I hold my fist out for him to bump. "Good job on the goal last night."

I lean over and plant a kiss to Granny's forehead before depositing Ollie next to her. "Sorry for missing you this morning. It won't happen again."

She looks surprised. "It's okay. Issi said you had an early meeting."

I blink at her. Right. Of course Issi covered for me.

I turn and walk over to my brother and Issi. "Brother," I say to Ford before muscling him out of the way. "I'm cutting in."

He just smirks and walks away as I take Isabella into my arms.

She tries to resist me, but I hold her tighter. "Dance with me, Bella."

Her eyes widen at the nickname, but at least she's not trying to pull out of my arms any longer. I know I shouldn't ask or even say anything, but jealousy is coursing through my veins. "You and Ford were looking awful chummy."

She won't look at me. She's looking over my shoulder instead. "He's nice to me," she answers.

I dip my head to force her to look at me. "And I haven't been." It's not an accusation or even a question. I know I haven't been nice to her, but I'm starting to realize that maybe I've been this way for a reason. I'm really good about not letting myself get close to people.

She doesn't answer me, and I spin her farther across the room away from Granny, Ford, and Ollie. "Do you like him? Do you like my brother?"

She doesn't answer me, and I say her name. "Bella, answer me."

Her long eyelashes flutter. "Do I like Ford? Of course, I do. He's a good guy."

I try to refrain from holding her even tighter than I already am. "So you want to date him?"

Her mouth falls open, and she whisper-hisses at me, "What is even wrong with you, Lucas? Yes, I like him but no, I don't want to date him. Your family really gets involved, don't they? I think I've answered more personal questions this week than I ever have in my life. Geez."

Finally, now after that reluctant reassurance, I feel a little better. "Okay, good. So you don't like Ford... not like that."

She rolls her eyes. "Yeah, you don't have to worry about me trying to force myself into the family or anything like that. I'm here to take care of G. That's it."

I slide my hands down her back, pulling her against me. The feel of her soft curves against my body has me thinking things I shouldn't be thinking in the presence of family, especially my nephew Ollie. With her breasts flattened to my chest, I caress my nose against the side of her neck and breathe her in. Her scent is pure seduction for me. I barely hold my groan in. "You feel good in my arms, Bella."

Her whole body trembles, and it thrills me to get that reaction out of her.

I sway back and forth with the music. "I should apologize to you for yesterday morning. I didn't mean to insinuate that you couldn't take care of Granny."

She shakes her head, but I don't let her pull away. Her voice is soft and timid. "No, you have every right to question me, Lucas. You're looking out for your grandmother, and no one could fault you for that."

I pull back and search her face. Her cheeks are tinged pink as she looks at me, but at least she's looking at me now instead of some random spot over my shoulder. "No, but no one should question your abilities either. Especially me. I see how much she means to you. I know you'd do anything for her."

She licks her lips, and with her face only inches

from me, the thought of leaning in and touching mine to hers is overwhelming. "Thank you for that, Lucas. That really means a lot to me."

I nod, transfixed on her lips. I'm about to ask her to meet me later so we can talk when the night nurse comes into the room.

"Well, it looks like a party in here!"

Isabella pulls from my arms and slides her hands down her thighs. She almost looks as if she's been caught making out or something the way her chest and cheeks are red. I let my gaze travel down her body, but I don't make it past her chest. Her nipples are tight, pressed against the front of her shirt as she turns to walk away from me. She approaches Betsy, the night nurse, and thankfully, Betsy doesn't seem to notice. Thank God, Ford is in the other direction. I definitely don't want him getting any ideas, and he would if he saw her like that.

I talk to Ford, Ollie, and Granny, and eventually Isabella comes over to hug Granny good night. She avoids looking at me, which is fine, but she does tell us all goodbye as she walks out of the room. I'm going to let her off the hook–for now, anyway.

Shortly after she walks out, Ford and Ollie leave too.

I help Granny to her bedroom, and she leans onto me heavily. "You doing okay?" I ask her.

She lets out a breath as she sits down on the edge of the bed. I know Betsy will be in to help her into her nightgown soon, so I sit next to her. "Yeah, I'm okay. I don't want you worrying about me, Lucas. You're young, and you should be living your life. Not stuck in some house night after night, worrying."

I could argue with her. It would be easy to do. But I know that's not what she wants to hear. "I was thinking... how do you think I could win over Isabella? I mean, I haven't exactly had any luck getting on the right foot with her."

The smile that lights up her face makes it all worth it. Yeah, I'm attracted to Isabella. Who wouldn't be? And I know nothing serious can come of it. But I know if I can just talk to her about it, she'd be game in pulling this off with me.

Granny claps her hands together. "I knew it. I knew I saw sparks when you two are together." She grabs on to my hand and squeezes it. "Well, first of all, you should probably ask her out for a date, don't you think?"

I laugh because of course Granny makes it all just sound so simple. "Yeah, a date. Good idea. I don't know why I didn't think of that. Maybe I'll ask her out on a date."

Granny squeezes my hand. "She'll say yes. I know she will."

I nod and smile at her as if I don't have a care in the world, but there is a part of me that wonders if Isabella may just say no to what I'm proposing.

CHAPTER 7

Isabella

I make it back to my room with my heart racing. I don't have any clue what has come over Lucas, but I don't know if I'm going to survive it. My heart won't for sure. He's playing some kind of game, and it looks like I'm his target. I'm not even sure what to think about him acting like he's jealous or something. None of it makes sense.

I change out of my scrubs into jeans and a T-shirt. Pulling my hair from its ponytail, I brush the long strands until they're shining. I need to get out of the house. Maybe I'll head into town and see if Carlotta wants to meet me. I haven't taken the time to see my best friend lately, and I know I need to catch up. I roll my eyes as I grab my purse. Knowing Carlotta, she's going to tell me to go for it. Whatever he's wanting, give it to him.

I get to my bedroom door and am about to pull it open when my phone dings.

I dig it out of my purse and almost drop it on the floor when I see it's a text message from Lucas. I stand frozen, staring at his name on my phone. *Don't open it.* That's what I tell myself, but I know I have to. He might need to talk to me about G.

I open the message app and scan his message.

Meet me in my office.

I'm holding it with both hands, and I keep reading it as if the five words are going to give me more detail of exactly what he's wanting. I'm about to tell him I'm on my way out when another message pops up. *Please. It will just take a few minutes.*

I groan, knowing I can't deny him. Heck, I can't even try and sneak out because his office is right next to the stairs. So unless I want to jump out of a window, I'm going to have to go and talk to him.

I text him back. *On my way.*

I pull my purse strap farther up my shoulder, take three deep breaths and walk out of my room. The whole way down the steps, I try to get myself prepared for whatever is about to happen. Is he going to fire me?

Kiss me? Hell, with everything the last few days, I don't even know what's going through his head.

Once I reach the landing, I walk up to his open office doors and knock on them. "You wanted to see me?"

He nods, and his gaze travels up and down my body. He smiles through narrow eyes. "Are you going out?"

I cross my arms over my chest because just standing across the room from him does things to my body that I don't know what to do with. Does he know I'm attracted to him? His granny told him I loved him, but does he think she was just making it up? I definitely don't need to let my body betray me now. I try to remain aloof, as if his summoning me has no effect on me. "Yeah, I'm going to the Whistler."

I name the only bar in Whiskey Run. It's a good bar with a dance floor, and Carlotta and I have spent a lot of evenings unwinding there.

He tilts his head to the side. "Alone?"

My eyes widen for just a second until I pull myself together. "No, I'm meeting someone."

He frowns at me but gestures at the couch in his office. "Have a seat."

I unfold my arms and sit down on the couch at the

very edge. My butt barely hits the leather and I'm blurting out, "Are you firing me?"

He seems taken aback. "No, I'm not firing you. I'm not sure why you would think that, but I guess I need to deal with that first. No, Isabella, I'm not firing you today, tomorrow, or any time in the future. I have no intention of letting you go. You make my grandmother happy, and you take really good care of her. I know I've given you grief, but that's on me. We are very happy with the work you do here."

I let out a sigh of relief, and it feels as if a weight has been lifted off my shoulders. "Okay, good, because I really want to be here for Lottie. And even if you did fire me, I'd still be here. I can't just leave her."

He nods and sits down next to me. We are not touching, but I swear I can still feel the heat from his body. "Well, it's a moot point. You're not fired, but I appreciate your loyalty to my grandmother. The reason I wanted to talk to you is because I want to make you a proposition."

My eyes widen, but I sit completely still. I refuse to let my mind wander because I can't even begin to guess what this could be about. Yeah, he's been acting weird lately, but what does that have to do with me?

Whatever it is, he's not happy about it. That much is obvious. "What is it?"

He doesn't even blink. "I want you to marry me."

My mouth drops open, and I gasp at the same time. Of everything I thought he'd say, that wasn't anywhere on the list, that's for sure. I try to keep it together and stutter back to him, "You want me to marry you?"

He nods. "Yes. My grandmother is worried about me, and I recently found out that if I marry you, her worry will be gone."

I shake my head because none of this makes sense. "Yes, she's worried about how you'll take her passing, but you getting married is not going to fix that, Lucas. She doesn't want you to get married just because that's what you think she wants. She wants you to love and be loved by someone. She wants to know that you've opened your heart again. She wants to know that when she's gone, you have someone unconditionally by your side."

He runs his hands through his hair and then across his face before squeezing the bridge of his nose. "Well, I don't have time for all that, and you know it, Isabella. I don't have much time left, and I thought that knowing how you feel about Granny, you would be willing to help me out."

"She'll know it's not real."

He lifts his shoulders. "We'll have to show her it is.

What? Can you not act like you love me for a few months?"

I bite my lower lip. My heart is wrenching in my chest because he thinks he has months with his grandmother, but I know that her time is even more limited than that. But I can't tell him that. "What about you? Can you do that?"

"Yes," he says, but by the look on his face, he's not even convinced of it himself.

I shake my head and squeeze my hands together in my lap. "No one is going to believe you've just fallen in love with me, Lucas."

He shrugs as if it's no big deal. "I can be convincing."

If only this was real. Already I can feel my heart breaking in my chest. There's no way I can play this game and come out unscathed. I'm about to tell him no when he leans forward. "I have a contract already put together. I can pay you to be my wife."

I jump out of my seat and stand over him. Surprise and shock floods through my body, and I say the first thing that comes to my mouth. "Fuck you, Lucas Blaze."

I turn to walk out, knowing I need to cool down when his hand circles my wrist. "Stop. I'm sorry. Fuck, I'm sorry, Bella. It's not like I've ever done this before, and obviously I'm not handling things the right way. Listen, forget the money…"

I spit the words at him. "Yeah because I'm not a prostitute."

His brows lift, and he tugs me toward him. "Look, I know. Or I should have known you wouldn't take any money. All I'm saying is that I want the time Granny has left to be in peace. That's all. I don't want to live with the guilt knowing that she's worried about me… and about you."

A lump forms in my throat. "Me?"

He nods. "Yeah, she said she's worried about you too, Isabella. She knows you won't have anyone when she's gone."

Pain shoots through me like a pinball. My grandma is gone, and so are my mom and dad. He's right. I won't have anyone when G leaves us, but Lucas has to know what Lottie is doing. I pull my wrist from his hold and grab on to both of his forearms. "Lucas, listen, you know she's just trying to fix us up, right? In her head, you and I make sense, and she's just trying to play matchmaker."

He nods. "I know all that. I also know that she's eighty-one years old. Let's give her what she wants."

"Have you mentioned this to Kelly?"

He scrunches up his eyebrows thoughtfully. "My assistant?"

I nod, and at the same time, he shakes his head. "No, but I don't see what she has to do with this."

Surely he knows how his assistant feels about him. "She's not going to like it."

He's looking at me, his face unreadable. "I don't care."

I realize that I'm still holding on to his arms, and I release him quickly before taking a step back. "Can I think about it?"

He doesn't let me get far. "Of course you can, but we don't have long."

I nod in understanding and leave the room in a hurry. Instead of going to the front door, I run up the steps and don't let out a breath until I'm in my room behind closed doors. I lean back against the hard wood and look at the ceiling. I know if I want to keep my heart intact, I need to tell him no. But how can I?

CHAPTER 8

Lucas

I wanted to demand an answer from Isabella, but I knew I couldn't. I was asking a lot from her, and I needed to give her time to think about it. So when Austin texted me right after she left and asked me to go to Jasper with him to meet with a potential client, I said yes. I made sure to tell Granny goodbye so she wouldn't expect me in the morning, and I met Austin at the distillery so he could leave his car there.

The drive to Jasper was short, and we met the client at the hotel restaurant. He's only in town until the morning.

We met with the client for a late dinner, and everything went smoothly. Usually this was my department, but this is one of Austin's contacts that he made when he was in college. I guess I came for the moral support.

After a successful dinner, Austin and I make our way to the bar at the same hotel. Austin is on his second shot as I nurse my first beer since I keep getting lost in thought. I asked someone... fuck, not just anyone–I asked Isabella to marry me. I wait for the panic to settle over me, but it never does. Maybe it's because I know it's fake and it's not going to last. I'm doing this for Granny.

Austin's smile drops from his face, and he throws his hands up and yells at me in the loud bar. "All right. What's up? What's going on with you?"

I lift the beer bottle to my lips. "Nothing is going on with me."

Austin shakes his head and looks at the women standing at the table next to us. "Well, smile. Act like you're having a little fun." He nods at a pretty blonde before looking back at me. "Get your game face on, brother. Incoming."

He barely gets the words out and the two women come over to our table. The brown-haired woman comes to stand next to me and bats her lashes. "Hi."

My first thought is that her hair reminds me of Isabella's. It's long and straight too. But that's where the similarities stop. "Hi," I mutter to her.

I take another drink of the warm beer. I'm not normally an asshole, and this time last week, I'd probably entertain the idea of whatever this woman is offering, but today there is no part of me that's interested. But the woman doesn't seem to take the hint.

She slides closer to me and presses the side of her breast to my arm. "It's loud in here. You want to go somewhere so we can talk?"

I shake my head. "No."

She laughs but doesn't take the hint. I stand awkwardly. I don't want to be a complete dick, but I'm about to be. "I'm going to get out of here," I tell her before turning to my brother. "Hey, I'm going to the room."

I walk off and out into the lobby when my brother catches up with me. "What the fuck, Lucas? And don't tell me nothing. Something's going on in that head of yours. What is it?"

I sigh and turn the key card to the hotel room over in my hand. "I asked Isabella to marry me today."

His mouth drops open, and before he gets any weird ideas, I tell him, "I did it because that's what Granny wants. She's worried about me, which I don't understand. You're the one hooking up at bars and dating women left and right, not me. But hey, whatever."

Austin crosses his arms over his chest. "First of all, I don't hook up left and right. What did she say?"

I shrug and hate to admit it, but I do. "She needed to think about it."

Austin lets out a big sigh and slaps me on the back. "Shew, thank God. Okay, tell her you changed your mind."

"What? I didn't change my mind. If she says yes, I'm doing it. I'm going to marry her."

He puts his face in his hand. "Fuck, Lucas, you can't marry her. You'll destroy her."

I shake my head in disbelief. What the hell do my brothers even think of me? "You're the second person to tell me this is a bad idea and I'm going to hurt Isabella. What is it you all know about me that I don't because as far as I know, I never go around hurting women."

He puts his hands on his hips. "Not on purpose, you don't. Fuck, Lucas, it's your MO. You hook up, and it's never anything serious. The woman knows she's going to get a good time out of it, no strings attached. But Isabella is not that way. She loves you, and you're going to hurt her. She's already a part of this family. Don't. Do. It."

I can hear by the tone of his voice how strongly he feels about this, and I try to reassure him. "Granny…"

He cuts me off. "Granny will be fine. Yeah, she hates that you've got your heart guarded like Fort

Knox, but that doesn't mean she wants you to use Issi–"

"I'm not using Issi. I told her everything up front. There's no expectations. She knows the deal."

He shakes his head in frustration. "There's no talking you out of this, is there?"

I fold my arms across my chest defensively. "No. No, there's not. If Bella says yes, then we'll be getting married."

I wait for him to argue with me some more, but he doesn't. "You'd better be completely honest with her. Promise me you'll tell her the complete truth. That this whole thing is fake, and you'll never love her. She needs to know it all before she gives you an answer. At least give her that, Lucas."

I nod in agreement. "I promise."

Austin sighs loudly, "Fuck, I need a drink."

I point at the bar. "Looks like you just left that and a woman in there. I'm going up to the room. I'm leaving early in the morning. With or without you, fucker."

He smiles, already forgetting our disagreement, but that's the way Austin is. "I'll be back before dawn."

I turn on my heel and head to the elevators, punching in the button.

The whole ride to the second floor, I'm thinking about what Austin said. I no sooner get to the room and sit on the bed before I'm pulling my phone out and texting Isabella.

Hey. Did you go to the Whistler?

I don't know why, but it hits me that I didn't ask her who she was meeting. Hell, I didn't even ask her if she's seeing anyone. She could have had a date, for all I know.

I wait for the response, and when I see the tiny dots letting me know she's typing something, I hold my breath. *No, I stayed in. You gave me a lot to think about.*

I didn't mean to ruin your night, I tell her, but as soon as I hit send, I know I'm lying. I don't like the idea of her dating, but I blame it on the fact that she may be my wife soon. Of course we won't be able to pull it off if she's seeing someone.

You didn't ruin it.

A small smile forms on my lips. *I won't be there in the morning. I'm in Jasper with Austin. I told Granny so she won't miss me.*

The bubbles appear but then disappear. I wait, but when nothing comes through I start typing again. *I'll see you tomorrow.*

She's slow to text back, but when she finally does, it's short and to the point. *Yeah. Have a good night.*

I don't know why, but ten minutes later, I'm still staring at the phone. I want more from her, and it's probably more than I have a right to ask for. I want her answer to my proposal, and I want it to be yes. Everything inside me says to text her and pressure her for that yes, but I know that's not the right thing to do. I can blame this urgency I'm feeling on borrowed time, but I know it's more than that.

Finally, I text her back. *You too, Bella. Have a good night.*

CHAPTER 9

Isabella

It's late afternoon, and I'm still thinking about Lucas and his proposal. His text last night surprised me when he told me that he wouldn't be here this morning. I know he didn't have to check in with me, and it's really none of my business, but I appreciated knowing so I didn't have to try and cover for him this morning with Lottie.

But even with all that, I can't help but wonder what he is doing in Jasper and who he is spending his time with. I almost typed the question out but thankfully caught myself in time. I have a feeling he wouldn't appreciate my nosiness, and right now, I'm his granny's nurse. I have no right to ask who he spends his time with. But the question remains: If I do marry him, would I have the right then?

I've thought of nothing else since last night, and I know I need to talk to him and ask him my questions. It's late afternoon when I hear him bounding up the steps. I keep my eyes averted as I pull out the medication that G needs to take. I concentrate, wanting to make sure I don't make a mistake. With the heart medication she's on, I double- and triple-check everything.

When I have it together, I turn just as Lucas is bending over to give Lottie a hug. "How you feeling, Granny?"

She smiles at him, but it doesn't quite reach her eyes. She's deteriorating more and more every day. I see it, and I watch Lucas to see if he's noticing or not. By the downturn of his lips, he does. "We may have to skip the dancing for a while. What do you think?"

She looks between me and Lucas. "Maybe, but I could always watch you and Isabella dance."

He laughs, and I take my cue to walk over and hand her the cup of water with her medication. "Time for your meds, G."

She takes them without argument, and after she drinks half the glass of water, I set it on the table next to her.

I'm standing next to Lucas when I feel his hand snake around my waist. I suck in a breath at the unexpected contact, but Lucas doesn't act as if he notices. If anything, he pulls me in closer, and I can feel the heat of his body at my back. He's so close I can feel his breath on my cheek when he asks his granny, "Can I kidnap Bella? I want to take her for dinner."

Granny lights up, and I hate to admit it, but it's the most animated she's been all day. She's practically shooing us out the door. "Absolutely. You two have fun."

But I'm rooted to the spot. The night nurse hasn't gotten here yet. "Betsy–"

But as soon as I say her name, she comes through the door of G's suite. "Betsy is here. You kids have fun."

"I need to grab my purse."

He nods. "I'll wait for you downstairs."

I nod and look down at myself in my jeans and T-shirt. "Do I need to change clothes?"

He shakes his head. "No, you look perfect, Bella."

Again, I try to ignore the nickname he's given me and rush off toward my room. I freshen up my mascara and lip gloss and run a brush through my hair before grabbing my purse and meeting Lucas downstairs.

He's watching me closely, and I know he's wondering if I've made a decision. "This is a good idea... to talk, I mean. After yesterday... I have a lot of questions."

"Is Red's okay for dinner?"

He names the busiest restaurant in Whiskey Run, but it's not like there are a lot of options. "Yes, that's fine."

It only takes minutes for us to get to the diner and get seated. We both stumble through ordering, and it's not until we've said hi to half the town who are here too for dinner before Lucas gets to it. "Before you give me your answer, I feel like I need to explain something."

I put my hands on the table in front of me. "Okay."

He pulls at the collar of his shirt. "So when I asked you to marry me... I don't want you to get the wrong idea."

"Okaaaay... explain."

He's obviously uncomfortable. "I just mean that you know me. Marriage is not my thing, and I don't want you thinking that this is a forever kind of thing."

I sit back and let my hands fall to my lap. This is definitely not going how I thought it would. "Okay, so you're thinking that because you asked me to marry you that I would think that you what? Fell in love with me or something? Trust me, I know my role in this. I know why you're doing this, and I know there is an end to it. I don't have the wrong idea."

He sighs and visibly relaxes. Talk about a gut check to the ego. Damn. "Okay, so I guess now is as good as time as any to talk about the dos and don'ts of this, right?"

The waitress brings our drinks to the table, and even though she has eyes for Lucas (who can blame her?), he continues looking at me. When he tells her thanks, she walks away, and he takes a gulp of his water. "Okay, so terms of our agreement. It's simple enough. While we're married, you'll be faithful."

I try to hold it in, but a laugh bursts from me. "Okay."

He shakes his head like he thinks I'm joking or something. "I mean it, no dating or other men."

I resist rolling my eyes. "Got it. I can do that... or I guess I should say not do that." Damn, he doesn't realize how easy that one will be for me.

He continues, "And Granny will have to believe it. She'll need to believe you love me and that we're unable to resist our attraction to each other."

I am drinking my tea when he says that one, and I almost choke on it. "Okay," I mutter.

"Are you okay?" he asks me.

I nod. "Yeah, so here are my questions. Are you

going to be faithful? I mean, are you planning on dating or whatever it is you do while we're married?"

"No."

I look at him skeptically.

He looks offended. "What kind of man do you think I am? If I'm married to you, I'm not going to be going out with other women or anything."

I lean forward and talk low. All we need is for the town gossips to hear our conversation. "What do you expect me to think, Lucas? You're telling me that this is a fake marriage. I know you don't normally bring women to your house, but all I'm saying is that I don't want to be made a fool of either. If you're going to see other women, then I just want a heads-up. I want to know before I commit to anything."

He reaches across the table and grabs on to my hand. "I promise you... I will be faithful."

I stare at his two hands wrapped around mine before meeting his eyes. "How many people are going to know this is fake... or a marriage of convenience or whatever you want to call it?"

"My brothers, and that's only because they know everything I do. To everyone else, this will be a real marriage."

I pull my hand from his because it's hard to think while he's touching me. I hate to even bring up her name, but I'd be amiss if I didn't ask about his assistant. "And Kelly?"

"To anyone else, this is real."

I can feel my cheeks go hot. "And how real are you talking?"

He pulls at the collar of his shirt again. "I've thought about that. If we're going to convince Granny this is real, we need to sleep together, but we're grown adults. I'll stay on my side, and you'll stay on your side."

I need him to spell it out. "So no S-E-X."

He laughs at that. "Bella, why are you spelling it?"

I lift my shoulders to my ears in embarrassment. When I don't respond, he leans forward and whispers, "Have you thought about it? Having sex with me, I mean?"

My pulse hammers in my throat.

I'm saved from answering when the waitress brings our dinner and sets the plates down in front of us. I busy myself unrolling the silverware and putting the napkin in my lap before digging in like I can't wait to eat.

Lucas breaks the silence. "I've thought about it... with you, I mean."

I drop my fork and stare at him. He didn't just say

what I thought he said. My mouth is hanging open, and he points at my plate with his fork. "Eat."

I dutifully pick up the fork, but I'm still staring at him.

He starts to cut the steak on his plate, and thank goodness he's not looking at me when he confesses. "What? Look at you. How could I not think about it?"

I lean back and look down at myself. Once I get past the too-large chest that people tend to stare at, I find the same wide hips that I curse every day when I have to tug the jeans over them. Same soft middle. I lift my eyes and look at him, not understanding.

His eyes are open wide in surprise. "Well, I'll be... you don't know, do you?"

I gulp. "Know what?"

He leans forward, and so do I because I'm really curious now. He looks at my chest, and a big smile forms on his face. "I'm just going to say it, Bella. You have a body made for fucking."

My whole body jerks in reaction. That has to be the hottest thing anyone has ever said to me. I put a hand to my chest. "Uh, what...?"

He nods, and his eyes turn a shade darker. "Yeah, honey. I'm sure I'm not the only person to tell you so, but when a man looks at you–"

He cuts himself off and shakes his head before

leaning back. He sets down the knife in his hand and pulls at his collar again. "Damn, it's hot in here."

I nod my head in agreement because I'm pretty sure my whole body just had a hot flash. He takes a bite of his steak and looks at me with regret. "But of course, we can't do that. That would confuse things when it ends."

I take a bite of the steak in front of me, but it tastes like sawdust to me. "Right... when it ends," I repeat. Like I was doused in cold water, I'm brought back to reality. Basically, Lucas wants to fuck me... but he doesn't want forever. I should probably ask more about what's going to happen when this ends, but I don't.

The rest of the meal, we have a normal conversation, staying off the topic of the marriage. It's not until we pull into the driveway later and get out to walk inside that I grab his hand. "All right... I'll do it. I'll marry you... for G."

CHAPTER 10
Lucas

She keeps walking as if she didn't just drop a bomb. I put my finger through the belt loop of her jeans and tug her to a stop. In amazement, I ask her so there's no confusion, "You'll marry me?"

She shrugs. She's biting her lip, trying not to smile, and I thread an arm around her waist, pulling her to me. Finally, she answers me. "Yes. I'll marry you."

"Saturday."

She puts her hands to my chest and leans back so she can see my face. "Saturday? This Saturday?"

I nod, fighting with myself not to lean down the few inches and kiss her.

"Lucas, that's crazy. We can't pull this off by Saturday. No one is going to believe that we've fallen in love overnight and are now getting married THIS SATUR-DAY. No way. It's too soon."

"Chicken," I tease her, and her hands clench on to my shirt. I know she can't stand a dare.

"Chicken? I'm not a chicken, but think about it, Lucas. You want this to be believable. No one is going to believe it."

I shrug. "We tell people we've been secretly dating for six months. People want to believe in love, Bella. They'll want to believe it."

She bites her lip, and everything inside me wants to put my lips to hers to soothe the tender skin. I put a hand on her hips and tug her against me. "What do you say?"

She looks at me doubtfully. "You think you can convince people you want to marry me? That this isn't some kind of game?"

I lean forward and press my lips to her forehead. "Abso-fuckin-lutely."

She shrugs. "Okay, let's do it."

I wait for panic to hit me, but it never comes. Really the only thing I feel is a deep longing. I slide my hands from her waist to her back so I can hold her in place. "So it's a deal?"

She laughs. "Yeah, deal. Should we shake on it?"

The smile drops from my face. I don't want to

shake on it, but I'm probably going to hell for what I say next. "We should probably kiss on it. We do need to be convincing, right?"

She licks her lips as her eyes search mine. "Right. Practice would probably be a good idea."

I press my lips to hers. I meant it to be a small peck, something to warm us up to each other so we're not so awkward in the coming days, but that idea goes straight out the window as soon as my lips touch hers. I nip at her, and she moans, giving me full and complete access. I waste no time and slide my tongue along hers, tasting her for the first time. Cupping her jaw, I tilt her head to the side so I can deepen our kiss. I should pull away, but I can't. With her hands stroking up and down my chest, my whole body reacts, and I slide my hands down her back, cupping her ass cheeks and pulling her into my body. I know she can feel my arousal, but I don't care. She feels way too good, and I never imagined kissing her would be like this.

I could do this all night until I hear a car door slam from somewhere in the neighborhood. She pulls back, but I don't let her go far. Her eyes are wide and her lips swollen. I still have my hands on her ass, but I don't want to move them. "I don't think we'll have any problem fooling anyone."

The light in her eyes dims, and I want to kick

myself. That definitely wasn't what she was wanting to hear.

"Uh, right. Yep. Good practice. I'm going to go on to bed. Early day tomorrow."

I want to stop her or ask her to talk some more, but I know it's best to let her go. I need to pull myself together.

I let her go in and walk up and down the driveway a few times to get my head on straight.

When I make it inside, the lights are off, and I make it as far as my office. I don't trust myself to not go upstairs and knock on Isabella's door so we can finish what we started.

I force myself to work for hours, and I sleep for a little while on the couch in my office. Bright and early the next morning, I shower and send a text to Kelly that we're working from my house the rest of the week. I make a point to see Granny before Isabella comes on shift, and I am back in my office working all morning.

Right before lunch, I realize that I need to talk to Kelly. "Hey, there's something I need to talk to you about."

She nods, crossing her legs. Her skirt rides up her thighs, and I don't want to give her any ideas, so I keep busy as if I'm straightening things on my desk. I decide straight and to the point is the best way to do this. "I'm getting married."

She bolts from her chair and stands up, coming to my desk. "Excuse me. You're what?"

Okay, I knew she would be surprised, but I wasn't expecting this. "Yeah, I'm getting married to Isabella."

She flinches, and a look of pure disgust crosses her features. "You're marrying your grandmother's nurse? Is this a joke?"

She laughs but stops when she sees the stern look on my face, and then she shakes her head as if she doesn't believe me. "Lucas! You have to be kidding me. You could do so much–"

I cut her off by holding my hand up. "Don't even think of finishing that sentence."

At that exact moment, there's the sound of shoes walking down the hall, and I make my way to the door. All I see is Isabella's back as she rushes away. "Bella."

She stops and freezes, and I know she wishes she hadn't been seen, but now is as good as time as any to show her that we can do this. If Kelly hasn't ruined it. "Come here, Bella."

She turns to look at me, her eyes wide. She doesn't want to come. She looks as if she'd rather run than anything, but she drops her head and makes her way to me. I want to meet her halfway, but I know if I stay where I'm at, Kelly will get to see exactly what I feel for my future wife. I put a finger to Bella's chin and lift it up so she's looking at me. "Morning, sweetheart."

She smiles, but it doesn't quite reach her eyes. *Damn you, Kelly.* "You're working from home today?" she asks me.

I nod. "Yeah, we have a lot to plan by Saturday, and I thought it would be better if I did it from here. Plus, you know I hate to be too far from you. I don't want to give you any time to change your mind." As soon as I say it, I know it's the truth. Now, more than ever, I want this to happen.

She nods, and I do what I've been thinking about doing all last night and again this morning. I cup her cheek and mold my mouth over hers. I don't hold back. I want her to know that I don't care what Kelly thinks–or anyone, for that matter. I feel a panic even while we're kissing, and the only thing that soothes it is when Isabella moans and pulls me closer. I gather her in my arms and pull my lips from hers breathlessly. "I've got a few things to finish and then I'm going to come upstairs and have lunch with you and Granny."

She nods wordlessly.

She walks away, and I turn to Kelly, who's standing in my office watching with her mouth hanging open.

"Do you want me to ask Bridget to bring you lunch in here?"

Kelly shakes her head. "No, I think I'll go into town for lunch."

I nod, and instead of going to finish anything, I go up the steps toward Granny's wing of the house. As soon as I walk into the room, I walk straight for Isabella and pull her against me. I lean down and kiss her neck. "Did you tell her?"

Granny looks between the two of us. "Tell me what?"

Without hesitating, I tell her, "I asked Bella to marry me, and she said yes."

Granny looks between the two of us, happiness shining on her face. She grabs a tissue off the table next to her. "Oh my, wow, that's wonderful news." She points her look at Bella. "And you, Bella, are you happy?"

Bella turns and wraps her arms around my middle. "You know I am, Granny."

I figure I might as well get it all out on the table. "And we're getting married this Saturday."

"Saturday?" Granny exclaims. "That's too soon. We'll never be able to plan a wedding that quickly."

I lace my fingers with Bella's. "We both want a small wedding with just our families, Granny."

She still can't believe it. "Yeah, but Bella, you should get the wedding of your dreams." She leans forward and looks at us worriedly. "You're doing it so quick because of me, aren't you? You don't have to rush it. Just knowing you have each other is enough."

It's an out. I can tell her I agree, and Isabella and I can date for a while. Obviously, Granny is happy just having us together. I can feel Bella's gaze burning into me, and when I look down into her face, I can see she's giving me an out, but I can't do it. I don't want to. I lean down and press my lips to her forehead before turning to my grandmother. "No, Granny. I've waited too long as it is. I'm ready for Bella to be mine."

She is thrilled and tries to stand to hug us. We both walk over to her and lean over to hug her. The next few hours are filled with wedding talk and plans.

Isabella

"Married? Right! Har, har, Issi."

I nod my head without even a hint of a smile. I look into the face of my best friend, and unease settles over me. She thinks I'm crazy. I know she does. There's a part of me that wonders if it's partly true. This is all happening so fast. "I am, Carlotta. I'm getting married Saturday. And I want you to be my matron of honor."

She smirks, and when I still don't laugh, she shakes her head. "Wait. You're serious right now?"

I nod.

She looks around at the people at the bar drinking and having a good time around us. When she realizes she's not being punked or something, she asks, "I'm sorry, Issi, but you haven't even mentioned dating anyone. Who is this mysterious groom that you're supposed to be marrying Saturday?"

I can tell by her tone she doesn't believe me, and I can't say I blame her. Hell, last week we sat at this very bar–this very table–and I complained that I was going to die a virgin. "Lucas Blaze."

Her mouth falls open, and she slams it shut. "What the...? You're not kidding."

I slowly shake my head and stutter, "No, I'm not kidding." Hell, I can't blame Carlotta. I'm having a hard time believing it myself.

She scoots to the edge of her seat and grabs my hand. "Okay, what have I missed? Did he realize he's dying of love for you? Did you tell him if he wants the *you know*, he has to put a ring on it first? Way to go, girl, if so. Very smart."

I shake my head. I know we agreed that we're not telling anyone that this is fake, but when Lucas said his brothers were coming over this evening, I told him that I would have to tell Carlotta the truth. I'm not worried, though, because I know she can keep a secret. Even one as good as this one.

I grab on to her forearms to try and calm her down a little. "Okay, so here's the deal, and don't freak out."

Her eyes widen, and I force the words out. "It's a fake marriage." I lower my voice. "I mean, we're really getting married, but not for the normal reasons and all that. We are only getting married for his granny. She's worried about him... heck, she's worried about both of us, and this is–"

Carlotta twists her arms and then grabs my hands. "This is crazy is what this is. I'm sorry, Issi. It's nice he wants to do this for his granny, but I don't want you to get hurt in all this."

I sigh because I knew that Carlotta would take it this way. She's my best friend and is always looking out for me. The waitress comes by, and I stop her. "Two shots of tequila and a beer. Whatever's on draft is fine."

She nods and walks away before I turn back to my friend.

"The tequila's for me, right?"

I laugh. "Yes, one for you and one for your hubby. You said he was coming, right?"

She nods. "Yeah, he's having someone drop him off so he can drive us home. So since he's going to be designated driver, the two shots are for me, and it sounds like I may need them."

I laugh because how could I not at this point? "Right. So I've already committed. I've said yes. He went and picked out rings today. He had someone take my measurements and is having a dress delivered later this week. Flowers have been ordered and catering arranged. I can't back out now, and quite honestly, I don't want to."

"Isabella," she says, and I know that tone. She's worried about me. She wants to be my voice of reason when usually I'm the one doing that job for her.

"I'm fine. I'm going to be fine. I want to do this. Trust me, I've thought about it, and I want to do this." I hold my hands up when she tries to argue with me. "Listen, you don't understand. Please don't be worried about me. I promise I'm going to be okay. You should have seen G when we told her we were getting married. I've never seen her so happy... so heck, Carlotta, she's dying, and it's happening fast. If I can make this any easier for her, make her feel like everyone is going to be okay when she goes, give her some peace, I have to do it."

The waitress brings back the drinks and moves them from her tray to the table in front of us. I put some cash on her tray and tell her to keep the change. Carlotta takes the first shot, and as soon as she swallows it, she slams her hand on the table with a sour look on her face. "Shew, I needed that. Okay, so I hate to be the one to bring it up, but you know I'm going to. What about your feelings for Lucas?"

There's no point in denying them. Not with Carlotta. "What about them?"

She grabs the other shot and holds it up. "You want this one?"

I shake my head. "No, I'm going to stick with the beer. I work tomorrow, and I need to keep my wits about me."

She nods and takes the second shot. "Well, I'm off tomorrow, and I didn't realize it before, but I do now. I obviously need this."

I take a sip of the beer as she chases her shot with a wedge of lime. I don't even try to change the subject because I know Carlotta, and she's not going to drop this. She makes the face again like I'm not sure if she swallowed fire or she's going to throw up, but she recovers quickly. "Okay, so you love the guy. You honestly think you can do this and keep your feelings in check? You think you can do this without getting hurt?"

I stare at her and try to weigh my answer before I start to speak. If anyone can see through my bullshit, it's Carlotta, and there's no way I can hide shit from her. Finally, I shrug my shoulders. "Probably not. Honestly, I know he's going to hurt me because the truth is, there's a part of me that wonders if we can make this work."

Carlotta reaches across the table and squeezes my hand while looking at me worriedly. I lean forward and tell her, "But I know that even though I'm hoping, it's not going to happen. Lucas Blaze"–I point at myself–"and me together doesn't make sense. Yes, we'll be married, and it probably won't be long, but I can't say no. I don't want to."

"He's a fool, you know."

I laugh, but we both know she's wrong because Lucas is actually a very smart man. "All I'm asking is for you to support me, Carl. Be there for me... and be my matron of honor. The rest of it we'll deal with as it comes."

She blows out a breath and rolls her eyes. "What color is my dress?"

I laugh. "I don't care. Any color you want."

She seems to think about it. "Red. Red looks good on me."

I nod in agreement. Red looks really good on her, but honestly, Carlotta is beautiful, and with her dark skin, she looks great in any color. "Yes, red would be perfect. And I know we won't have time to go shopping, so just send me what you want, and Lucas will order it."

She looks at me skeptically. "I'm not going cheap."

I roll my eyes. "It's fine. He won't care. I'm almost embarrassed for what he paid for my wedding dress."

"Oooh, girl, give me the details."

For the next two hours, we talk about the wedding. Dwayne eventually shows up and laughs as he has to help his wife out to the car. I sit in the back while Carlotta tells him all about the wedding. Everything is slurred, but it's funny. When we get back to Lucas and Lottie's house, Dwayne insists on walking me to the door when his wife tries to get out to do it.

"I guess she needed to let loose tonight."

He laughs. "Yeah, she never does, so when it happens, it's always an adventure."

We're both laughing when the front door opens. Lucas walks out onto the porch, his eyes moving between Dwayne and me.

"Hey, Lucas. This is Dwayne, Carlotta's husband. Dwayne, this is Lucas Blaze."

The two men shake hands, and we hear Carlotta hollering from the car, "Congratulations, Lucas! You better be good to my girl!"

Dwayne starts rushing back to the car. "See you all later. I better get her home."

Lucas hollers thank you to her, and we both wave. "I figured your brothers would be here still."

He points inside. "They are. Why did they bring you home? Is something wrong with your car?"

"Uh, no. Carlotta picked me up, and I had a couple of beers. She obviously had more." I laugh.

"Since neither of us should be driving, Dwayne was dropped off at the bar to drive us home."

He takes a step toward me. "Why didn't you call me? I could have come and picked you up."

I tilt my head to the side, unsure what the big deal is. "Uh, I knew your brothers were coming over."

He pinches his nose as if he's frustrated. "That doesn't matter. From now on, you call me." He jabs his thumb into his chest. "I'll pick you up."

I shrug and go to walk past him, and he grabs my arm. "Got it, Bella?"

I turn and put my hand on my hip. "Lucas, look. All this is new. I'm not sure what I'm supposed to be doing here. And honestly, until two days ago, there's no way I would ever had called you to come pick me up. For real, you would probably be the last person on the list, so I'm just trying to catch up here."

He blows out a breath and runs a hand through his hair. I hate it when he does that because put-together Lucas is hot, but hair mussed, exasperated Lucas is even hotter. "I know. I know. This is all happening quickly, and I don't know how everything is going to work either, but I do know that opening that front door and seeing another man walk you to the door—"

"He's my friend. He's my best friend's husband."

He shakes his head. "It doesn't matter. I didn't like

it. Just promise me from now on, you'll call me if you need a ride. That's all I'm asking."

There are so many questions rolling around in my head, but I don't dare ask them. "Sure. I can promise that."

He nods. "Good, so just a warning. My brothers are on the war path, so you may want to lay low."

Understanding smacks me in the face. "They don't want you to marry me. Did you tell them I'll sign a prenup and that I don't want anything out of this?"

He gazes down into my face. "No, surprisingly, none of that came up. They're mad at me for using you."

He turns to walk inside, and I follow behind him. At the stairs, I tell him I'll see him in the morning, and he gives me a once-over and a little nod before going into his home office. I'm at the first step when I hear the raised voices.

CHAPTER 12

Lucas

Finally, I've had enough. I throw my hands up in the air. "Listen, guys. I'm doing it. Nothing you can say is going to change how I feel about this. It's between Isabella and me, and we've both agreed to it. I'm not asking your permission or anything else. I'm asking you to be here on Saturday with smiles on your faces. That's all."

Austin, Ford, and Beau are all quiet, staring back at me. Hudson won't be here on Saturday because there's no way he'll be able to get leave on such short notice, but I have a feeling if he was here, he'd be trying to talk me out of it too. They're all so quiet, I think they're finally going to shut up about it when they all start talking at once.

I'm about to tell them to shut up when the office

door swings open, and Isabella is standing there looking at all of us. Her hair is in waves down her back, and her cheeks faintly pink. She quietly closes the door behind her. "Hey, guys, look I'm sorry to butt in, but if you keep this up, you're going to wake up your grandmother, and I don't think any of us want that."

They all agree, and I watch as Austin starts to walk toward her. Bella bypasses him and walks over to me. It's instinct to hold my hand out to her, and she takes it before turning next to me and facing my brothers. She's nervous. I know she is. And even though her voice shakes a little, she doesn't stop until she gets everything she wants to say out. "I appreciate... we appreciate that you guys want to look out for us. We know this is fast and maybe a little over the top, but after seeing your grandmother today when we told her the news, there's no way I can even think that we're making the wrong decision about this."

Ford takes a step toward us. "Issi, honey, you don't have to do this."

She pulls back her shoulders, and I slide my arm around her waist, pulling her closer to my side. I start to open my mouth, but she puts her hand to my chest. "Ford, Beau, Austin, all of you have been like big brothers to me, and I know you're just looking out for me. I know what this is. Lucas needs to do this for his grandmother, and after today, I see why it's so impor-tant to him. Now we're getting married with or without you there, but I'm telling you, all three of you had better be there because you will not only let down Lucas and me, you will devastate your grandmother. I will sign a prenup. I don't want anything from this marriage. Whatever he comes into it with, he's leaving with."

Beau pushes his glasses up on his head and holds up a finger. "Actually, Issi, it's only right you get paid something for your time–"

I mutter, "Fuck, here we go." I was on the receiving end the last time money was offered, and it wasn't pretty. I can already feel Bella tense next to me, and I try to soothe her by running my palm up and down her back.

Bella holds up her hand. "No, Beau. I don't want anything. She was my grandmother's best friend. She has been to every big event in my life, and after my grandmother passed, she continued to do so. She didn't have to do that. She... she's all I have left. I can't do anything else for Lottie, so please let me do this."

She's pleading with them. They all see it, and now so do I. I knew that my grandmother was important to her, but now I understand exactly how important. No one is going to argue with her. If they try, I'm going to kick them out.

Finally, Ford steps forward and hugs her, but I don't let her go. The other two take their turn, and through it all, I hold on to Bella.

Ford lifts his eyes to mine. "What do we need to do for Saturday? Whatever you need… we'll do it."

"I just need you in a black suit and to be here for the wedding with smiles on your faces. The story is that we've been dating for months if anyone mentions this is too fast, but honestly, it's just going to just be us on Saturday."

Ford nods and looks at Beau and Austin before turning to me. "You got it. We'll be here… all smiles."

"I'm going to walk them out. Stay here for a minute, will you?"

Bella looks surprised but agrees.

I walk my brothers out, and Ford hangs back. I'm hoping he's not going to try and talk me out of it in private. I've had enough for the night.

Honestly, I just want to get back inside with Bella. "All right, Ford, what is it? What do you have to say?"

He puts his hand on my shoulder and squeezes. "I just want to say that I see how you are with Issi." He shakes his hand in front of his face. "I mean, we all know how she feels about you, but tonight... I saw how you wanted to protect her–"

"I'm asking a lot of her, Ford. I know that."

He nods. "Yeah, you are, but it's more than that. You know what Granny always says. You need to be open to love. And when you find it, hold on to it."

"I know that. Hell, Ford, she's been telling us that since we were little."

He looks at the front door and back at me. "All I'm saying is you are so closed off. Hell, I've been through an ugly divorce, and you're more closed off to love than I am. I just want you to think about it. Could you have found it and not realized it yet?"

He squeezes my shoulder one more time. "I'll see you Saturday. Call me if you need anything before then."

It's not until my brother is in his car that his words hit me, and I understand what he's trying to tell me. Damn, I thought this would all be simple, but it's not simple at all.

I go back inside and make it to my office before closing the door behind me. Isabella has set down on the couch, and she looks at me when I come in. "You okay? Did they give you more crap about what we're doing?"

I move to sit next to her. "No. I think they've accepted it."

She nods. "That's good. Right? I mean you still want to do this, right? You still want to get married?"

She's watching me closely, and I put my hand on her knee. "Yeah, Bella. I still want to get married. That won't change."

She moistens her lip. "Why do you call me that? Everyone else calls me Isabella or Issi."

It's only now that I notice the glassy effect of her eyes, and I remember that she was drinking earlier. "How much did you have to drink?"

She looks up at the ceiling and back at me. "I had planned on one drink, but Carlotta talked me into having a second." She holds her hands up, and her beautiful eyes widen. "But don't worry. It was beer, nothing hard, and I'll be sober in the morning when my shift starts. I would never put G in any danger."

I push a piece of hair off her shoulder. "I know you wouldn't." I study her face and try not to get lost in the gold flecks of her dark eyes. "I call you Bella because it's a good name for you."

She scrunches her nose up and shakes her head. "No, it really isn't. I've tried to figure it out, and I'm thinking you're playing with me."

I rear back, surprised. "Playing with you? What do you mean?"

"You know. How they call the big guy Tiny. You're calling the frumpy girl beautiful. If that's the case, I'd rather you call me Issi... or even Isabella."

"I call you Bella because you're beautiful."

She starts to laugh, and I put my hand to her chin to make her look at me. It pains me to know that she thinks I've been making fun of her with the nickname. "Look at me, Bella."

She finally lifts her eyes to me. "You are beautiful, Bella. Both inside and out. The way you care for my grandmother, your friends, my brothers... for me."

She looks so sad, and it kills me that she doesn't believe a word I'm saying. "I wouldn't lie to you. You're beautiful, Bella."

It's like a mask drops over her face. She tries to hide every reaction from me, and I'm not having it. She lifts her shoulders in a shrug as if this conversation is over. "Okay, whatever, Lucas."

"Whatever, Lucas." I mimic her. "Listen to me. You're beautiful."

She puts her hand on my arm. "Stop, okay? You don't have to say that. You don't. I know what I am. I've seen the women you date, and I don't look anything like them. But I'm perfectly fine with who I am... I like who I am. If you say you're not making fun of me with the nickname, I believe you. Can we just drop it?"

Fuck me. She wants to drop it, and I should do as she asks. Her face is red. This conversation is obviously embarrassing her, but I can't let it go. I won't.

I pull her until she's sitting with her ass in my lap and her legs hanging to the side. She struggles, but I don't let her go. "What are you doing, Lucas? I'm too big to be sitting in your lap."

I laugh at first and then I groan because the more she moves, the more my body starts to react at having her near. "Stop," I demand.

She stops moving. Hell, I think she stops breathing. I circle my arms around her and pull her against my chest. "Breathe."

She lets out a breath, and I squeeze her hip. "I call you Bella because you're beautiful. I could say it's because of how you take care of Granny... or I can say it's because of what a good heart you have. Fuck, Bella, there's like a hundred things about you that make you beautiful because I mean you're beautiful. I like to look at you. I like to watch you dance. You make me think things I shouldn't fucking be thinking. And if you don't believe what I'm telling you... do you feel it? Can you feel my attraction to you? Because that's not something I can make up or force." I don't mean to be crude, but it's important to me that she understands. I lift my hips up, and there's no way she doesn't feel the hard proof of my desire against her hip. Her eyes widen when I raise up, and she puts her arms around my neck. I slide her up my lap even though it's painful. I won't stop though until she knows, and she believes me.

She nudges her hip a little, and her eyes widen even more. "You're...uh, you're uh, I mean..."

I lean in and whisper into her ear, "I'm hard, Bella. This is how I am with you. I know I shouldn't be. I know this could complicate things, and we can't act on it, but I need you to know that to me... you're beautiful."

She leans her head on my shoulder, and like a glutton for punishment, I revel in the feel of her curvy body pressed against mine. I can feel her everywhere, and it only excites me even more. I know I need to put some distance between us, and I will, but right now, I want something else. My voice is deep and thick. "Kiss me, Bella."

She slowly pulls back and searches my face. "We need to practice, right?"

I nod even though practice is not what I meant at

all. Fuck, I just need to have her lips on mine... that's all.

I wait for her to give me any sign of encouragement, and when she finally nods her head, I lean in to kiss her. I devour her mouth, tasting her, and when her tongue strokes against mine, I tilt my head to deepen the kiss. I get lost in the taste of her. She whimpers softly, and I move my hand to her rib cage, running it up and down under the curve of her breast. I can't take it, and when I cup her breast in my palm, she groans loudly. "Fuck," I grunt before pulling back to look at her. She's staring wide-eyed, and I continue to stroke my finger back and forth over her hard nipple. Her back arches, and I'm fighting with myself. I want to lift her shirt and fit my mouth over her breast. I want to suckle her... fuck, I want to do so many things to her. She's so damn responsive, and the only thing that stops me is knowing I can't fuck this up. I know me, and as soon as things get real, I want to cut loose. I can't do that to Bella. I fucking can't.

"Go, Bella. Go to your room before I do something that we'll both regret."

When she doesn't move, I lift her up and bring us both up to stand. My cock is so hard it's painful, but I know what I must do. I cup Isabella's face and stroke her cheek. She looks so confused right now, and I can't say I blame her. "Good night, Bella. I'll see you in the morning."

She bites her lower lip and walks away. She doesn't look back at me. Not when she opens the door, not when she walks out, and not when she passes by as she walks up the stairs. I reach between my legs and cup my hard cock through my pants. Fuck, how in the world does she not know she's beautiful? She's a fucking walking wet dream... and she's going to be mine.

CHAPTER 13

Isabella

Lucas thought of everything. The backyard has been turned into a beautiful oasis for the ceremony. There are red and white flowers everywhere. Someone brought in an arch that is breathtakingly beautiful. Everything is perfect.

"Are you sure about this, Issi? It's not too late. I can get Dwayne to pull the car around, and we can make a run for it."

I laugh because not many people would go against the Blaze family, but Carlotta doesn't seem scared at all. "No, I'm not changing my mind. But thank you."

She reaches for the veil on top of my head and adjusts it a little. "Girl, I'm glad you're going through with it because you make the most beautiful bride I've ever seen. If Lucas hasn't figured his crap out yet, he will when he sees you, that's for sure."

I turn and look at myself in the full-length mirror. I barely recognize the woman in front of me. Lucas spared no expense. He had makeup and hair artists here early this morning. This week has flown by, and Lucas has continued to work from home. I still think about that night in his office when he told me I was beautiful. I would do anything for a replay of that night, but he's kept his hands to himself since then. I'm trying to picture how this is all going to play out, and I gasp. "Oh no, I wasn't even thinking. I don't have anyone to give me away."

Carlotta's looking at me wide-eyed, and it's obvious she didn't think about it either. "Uhhhh," she stammers before snapping her fingers. "How about one of the brothers?"

I grab my phone off the counter and bring up the messaging app. "I'll text Lucas and see."

I type out a text. *Hey, I just realized I don't have anyone to give me away.*

I hit send and then type another one. *I mean, I can walk myself down. Forget it, I'll just do that.*

Bella, honey, you need to have someone walk you down to me.

I bite on to my lower lip. *I think there's a caterer here in a vest and bow tie, I can find a jacket for him.*

My phone rings, and it's Lucas. I answer it with a timid "Hey."

"Bella, honey, everything was getting screwed up on text, so I thought I'd call. You're not having some stranger give you away. Of course, if you want to walk by yourself you can, but it would mean a lot to me if you'd let Ford do it."

"But he's your best man."

He groans. "Don't let Beau or Austin hear you say that because they're still not happy about it. They've decided to ignore the fact that I asked Ford to be my best man. Anyway, he can walk you down to me and then stand by me. It's perfect... I mean, if that's okay with you."

I'm nodding into the phone and realize he can't see me. "Yes, that's fine. If you think Ford won't care."

"He'll be honored. So I'll see you soon? I won't need to chase you down or anything, right?"

I grip the phone tighter. "I'll see you soon."

I no sooner hang up the phone than there's a knock on the door. As Carlotta walks across the room to answer it, I tell her that Ford is going to walk me down the aisle. When she opens the door, the man himself walks in and stops when he sees me. "Wow."

I blush from head to toe.

"You look beautiful, Isabella. Absolutely stunning."

I reach for his outstretched hand. "Thank you. And thank you for walking me down the aisle."

He smirks at me. "My pleasure. I can't wait to see Lucas' face."

I look up at him. "What?"

He shakes his head just as music from outside starts to play. "Oh, nothing. I think it's game time."

Carlotta hands me a bouquet. "It's time, Issi. I'll see you down there, okay?"

I hug her, and she walks out the door. Nerves settle over me as I thread my arm through Ford's. "Second thoughts?" he asks.

"No. Not one."

"Good. I know it took me a little bit to get on board with this, but I think it's good. I think this is actually a really good idea."

Before I can ask him what changed his mind, the wedding march starts to play. Ford opens the door, and we walk the few steps to the aisle. I suck in a deep breath and start to walk. The whole way, I look at Lucas. I know we may not be getting married for the right reasons, but it feels right. Lucas is staring at me as if he's never seen me before, and he meets Ford and me before we even get to the end of the aisle.

Ford slaps him on the back. "In a hurry, brother?"

He takes my other arm and finishes the walk to the front. It takes a minute for the pastor to catch up, but finally he does. The ceremony is swift and over before I know it. I see G in the corner of my eye as she wipes her tears away, and when the pastor tells Lucas he may kiss the bride, I prepare myself but obviously not enough.

He leans me backwards and kisses me until I'm sure I hear fireworks going off. Imagine my surprise when there are actual fireworks lighting up the darkened sky. Everyone's eyes are on the sky except for Lucas' and mine. "Bella, my God, you're beautiful... and now you're mine."

I blink up at him, completely caught up in the moment. I know it's fake... I know it's all for show, but just for a minute, I let myself believe it's real. "And you're mine."

He nods and kisses me again. *This isn't real. This is fake.* I keep telling myself that over and over, but I'm having a hard time convincing myself of it because it's so easy to get caught up in all of it.

After the fireworks are over, everyone in attendance comes to congratulate us. It's when I finally make it to G that I sit down in the chair next to her and hug her. She whispers into my ear, "I know you and Lucas did this for me, and I love you for it, but I need you to promise me something."

I'm not going to argue with her or try to dissuade her. Lottie is a smart woman. "Anything."

She grips my hands with her frail ones. "Don't give up on him. It's going to take him awhile to figure it all out and realize what he has, but he will. I know my grandson, and he will."

I nod because it's an easy promise to make. I know that even when this is over and I'm forced to walk away, Lucas will always have a part of my heart. I know it. "I promise, G."

All of a sudden, Granny's favorite song by Usher starts to play over the speaker, and I can't help but laugh. "It sounds like they're playing our song, G."

Everyone gathers around G, Lucas, and me, and we have our own little dance party. Nothing about this wedding has been traditional, but I wouldn't change anything. Nothing at all.

Lucas

At the end of the night, after everyone has gone home and Granny is in her room at her wing of the house, Bella and I make our way upstairs. She's been quiet since everyone left, and I'm starting to feel the guilt settle in. When we get to the top of the stairs, Bella looks at me, unsure. "Well, good night. I guess I'll see you in the morning."

She's not looking at me, and she turns to go in the opposite direction before I reach for her. "I had Carlotta move all your things into my room today. I realize now that we never talked about it... I just assumed..."

I let my voice trail off, and she nods her head. "Right. I mean, of course you're right. We need to make this believable, and no one is going to believe it if we're newlyweds and sleep in different rooms."

I thread my fingers through hers and pull her toward the opposite end of the house where my suite is. As soon as we're inside, Bella starts to look at the room. There's a seating area with a couch, chair, and television. To one side of the room is the walk-in closet and bathroom, at the other side is the bedroom. I point to the closet. "All your clothes are in there."

She nods and points to the couch. "Do you want me to sleep there?"

I don't release her hand. "No, you can have the bed."

She rolls her eyes. "Lucas, I'm not kicking you out of your own bed. That's crazy."

I look at the double doors that lead to the king-size bed. "It's big. Surely we can both sleep there."

She gulps, and I realize that I'm making a lot of decisions and don't want her to be uncomfortable. "If you're not comfortable with any of this–"

But she cuts me off. "No, it's fine. It's not a problem. It's fine."

I nod as she pulls her hand from mine. "I'm going to go shower and change. Or uh, do you want the bathroom first?"

I shake my head. "No, honey, you go first. I'll take a shower down the hall."

She opens her mouth but closes it quickly with a nod before she walks off.

I take the coldest shower I've ever had in my life, and I make it to bed before Bella does. When she finally joins me, I can barely make her out in the dark as she climbs into the bed next to me. She has her back to me, and guilt is eating away at me. "I'm sorry about today. You deserve to have your dream wedding. I know this wasn't what you imagined. I should have done more."

She rolls over and faces me. I'd give anything to be able to see the look on her face. "It's fine, Lucas. Don't feel bad. It was good. Did you see the smile on G's face? That makes it all worth it."

I laugh out loud and shake the bed. "She loved that you chose rap music. I never would have thought I'd be dancing at my wedding to Nelly, Usher, and Tupac."

She laughs too. "It was perfect."

I almost slide my hand across the bed to hold hers but stop myself. "It was perfect, but I know you would have wanted something different. Don't think I didn't notice you picked all of G's favorite foods for the reception."

She can't take a compliment. "It's fine, Lucas. I loved it."

"Next time you get married, I'll pay for it."

Even as the words come out of my mouth, I feel almost sucker-punched because if we follow up with our plans, the chances are likely that she'll get married again.

Bella is quiet for the longest time, and I can tell the smile is gone from her face when she says, "That's okay. I doubt my husband would appreciate my ex-husband paying for our wedding. Thank you for the thought, though."

I roll onto my back and throw an arm over my face. I don't even want to think about Bella with another man. What was I thinking making that kind of offer? "I'll be honest with you, Bella. I can't believe you've been single as long as you have."

She hesitates for just a minute. "I, uh, guess the right man never came along."

I roll back toward her. "What's the right man? I mean, if you could make up the perfect guy, what would he be like?"

She lifts her arm and tucks her hands under her face. "Well, first of all, he wouldn't be perfect. I wouldn't want that. But he'd have to be a family man,

I'd want him to know what's really important in life. He'd have to be able to laugh and have a good time. Faithful. And love me... love me like he wouldn't want to go one day without me."

My voice is rough. "You want the fairy tale? It doesn't exist."

"It's not a fairy tale. Love like that exists. My mom and dad had that."

I feel guilty again that I've pretty much ruined marriage for her. I didn't think I'd feel this enormous guilt, but I do, and I can't seem to shake it.

"What about you? What are you looking for in a woman?"

I laugh and answer instantly. "A good time."

She doesn't respond except for a little hmmph.

"What?" I ask her.

"If you don't want to tell me, just say so. But don't expect me to believe that's the only thing you're looking for in a woman."

I groan. "Fine. If I ever settled down, I'd want a woman that wouldn't walk away."

"Not all women leave, Lucas."

I grunt a non-answer to her. There's no sense in going down this road because nothing she could say would convince me.

We're both quiet for a long time, and I begin to wonder if she's fallen asleep until she shakily asks, "Are you going to be able to refrain from sex during this, Lucas?"

Just her saying the word in my bed a few inches away from me has me hard. Already, I need another cold shower. I try to answer her without my voice squeaking. "Yeah, sure I am."

"Oh, I guess your trip with Austin the other day... I guess that will tide you over... I mean, it's none of my business."

I lift up on my elbow. "Wait, when I went out of town... What? You thought I hooked up with someone else?"

She doesn't answer me, but if I can't give her anything else, I can give her this. "Bella, honey, since the minute I had the idea to ask you to marry me, I haven't even looked at another woman. I'm not interested in anyone else, and I promised you I'd be faithful. I wasn't lying about that."

She moves, and I catch a glimpse of her face from the moonlight shining in the window. She's smiling, and it reminds me. "You were a beautiful bride, Bella. I couldn't take my eyes off you."

She smiles again, and I give up not touching her. I

reach across the bed and grab one of her hands. I lace our fingers together, and it's only then that I allow myself to close my eyes. "Good night, Bella."

She whispers back softly, "Good night, Lucas."

CHAPTER 15

Isabella

"What are you doing here? You just got married. You should be somewhere... anywhere... but here."

I laugh and walk farther into Lottie's room. "We are putting off the honeymoon for a few weeks. I didn't want to leave you, and it was sort of quick for Lucas to rearrange his schedule."

G holds her hands up. "No, I'm not having it. You can't stay here because of me. You should be living it up, enjoying each other, not staying in Whiskey Run tending to some old sick lady."

I go and sit in the chair across from her. "Nonsense. This is where we want to be, and don't be difficult because I have something you're going to want to see."

For the first time, G notices the iPad I'm holding, and she holds her hand out. "What is it? Let me see."

I laugh and lean over so I can show her the pictures. "Here you go. The photographer sent me pictures, and Carlotta sent me videos that she took last night. Just swipe right, and you can see them all."

Instead of looking at the pictures, I watch G's face as she looks at each one. She swipes again, and her face lights up. "Awwww."

I lean over to see which one she's looking at, and it's one of Lucas and me. Our family is all around us. There are fireworks in the sky, and I'm looking up at Lucas as if he is the only one there. Just looking at the picture makes me feel completely vulnerable.

G asks me softly, "You love him, don't you?"

"Of course I do, G. You know I do."

She's shaking her head before I even finish. "No, I mean for real. Not for show or because you're trying to make this ol' woman happy... you really love him?"

I can't lie to her. "Yeah, G. I love him. I shouldn't. I know he's going to break my heart, but yeah, this is where we're at."

She reaches for my hand, and her grip is so weak. "I don't know if you know the story of when Lucas was born."

I grimace. "Lucas never told me, but Ford mentioned it."

She nods. "Yeah, so to him, well, women leave, and they're not to be trusted. I know it's deeper than that, but that's the gist of it. His stepmom tried to help him, but when she married Oscar, she got five boys at one time. Lucas was the youngest and not in school yet, and he spent his days with me. I'm the only constant woman that's been in his life, and I haven't been the best example for him."

"G..."

She squeezes my hand a little tighter. "No, really, I haven't been. After my husband Paul died, I never settled down. I was a player of sorts."

I gasp. "G!"

She shrugs. "I was. I never settled down, and well, like I said, I wasn't a good example for him."

"He loves you, G. You know he does."

She nods. "I know he does. My point is that I don't want you to give up on him. It may take him awhile to figure it out, but I'm pretty sure his heart already loves you... He just needs to let his head catch up."

I can't tell her that this really is all fake or that there's no chance in hell that he'll ever love me. All I can do is nod my head and agree with her. "Sure, G. I know you're right."

She leans back and starts swiping through the pictures again.

"How are my two favorite ladies?"

Lucas comes striding in looking between his Granny and me. He's handsome in his navy blue pinstripe suit and crisp white shirt. He goes to his Granny first and kisses her on the forehead and hugs her. I can't help but wonder what all he heard before he came in here, but it's hard to tell because I feel like we're in an alternate universe when he comes to me next, leans down, and kisses me right on the lips. "Good morning, wife."

I almost choke out the words. "Morning."

He sits down next to me and puts his hand on my knee. "What are you two doing today?"

G sits up a little straighter, still holding the iPad to her chest. I doubt I'll get it back from her today. "I'm trying to convince your wife that she doesn't need to be here today. Heck, or the rest of the week. You should have taken her on a honeymoon, Lucas."

He nods. "I know, and we're planning one in a few weeks. We just did everything quickly, and you know how hectic it is at the distillery."

G knows all about the distillery. She ran it for years on her own until her son took it over. Now his sons are all running the show. "Yes, I know exactly how busy the distillery can be, but I also know that you have four–well, three other brothers that can pick up your slack... at least for a week. You didn't go because of me, and I'm not having it."

Lucas tries to hide his smile from her. "I know, G." He squeezes my knee. "Bella deserves a honeymoon, and I'm planning something amazing. I promise. I won't let either of you down. Okay?"

She begrudgingly agrees. "Fine. I just don't want either one of you to miss out on anything because of me."

"I know, Granny. I know." Lucas turns in his seat. "Can I talk to you in the hallway for a minute?"

I nod, and Granny starts to snicker. "Really? You think I don't know what's going on? You just want to be alone with her so you can kiss her. I'm hip on things, Lucas. I know all about being a newlywed."

He stands up and pulls me with him. "You got me, Granny. I can't get anything past you."

He threads our fingers together and pulls me toward the hallway. I look over my shoulder at G. "You better be good while I'm gone. I'll be right outside the door, and if I peek in here, and you're trying to stand up on your own, I'll, I'll... I'll delete all the rap music off my phone."

She gasps and smiles real big. "You got me. I'll stay right here."

Lucas and I are both laughing as we walk out into the hallway. We stop outside the door, and he moves his body so he's standing in front of me. "Is it okay if I go to the office for a little while?"

It's on the tip of my tongue to say sure when he continues. "Kelly called and said something came up that I need to see."

I try not to tense when he says his secretary's name. "Sure. Of course, whatever you need to do."

I try to keep the smile on my face and blink up at him. "Is that all? I should probably get back in there."

Before he can answer me, I turn to go only to have him wrap his hand around my arm and hold me to my spot. "Was there something else?"

He's looking at my mouth. "No, but we can't disappoint Granny. She thinks I'm out here ravishing you."

I can feel heat rise on my face. "Right. So you want me to stand here for a few minutes?"

He cups my face in his hands. "Yeah, something like that."

I bite on to my lower lip. He's looking at me like I'm his next meal or something. My stomach starts to flutter. "Lucas?" I say, even though I don't know for sure what I'm asking. I just know that looking into his eyes is doing something to me that I can't explain. I lift my hands and put my hands inside his jacket and grab his tucked-in shirt. He always looks put together and wrinkle-free, but that doesn't stop me from bunching the shirt in my hands.

He tilts his head to the side. "Bella, I'm thinking when you go back in there, you need to look as if you've been thoroughly kissed."

I can barely form a thought in my head; all I know is that Lucas is telling me he's going to kiss me. "Okay."

He doesn't waste any time. He leans down and covers my mouth with his. I press up on my tiptoes to get closer. My hands circle to his back, and I press my body against his. For someone that has never done a lot of kissing, I can definitely see the attraction of it all because damn, Lucas knows how to kiss.

His hands are still on my face, and he tilts my head before deepening the kiss. His tongue presses into my mouth, stroking me. I whimper at his touch, and he pulls back. His lips are swollen, eyes glazed over and hair mussed, and I'm sure I look the same, but I still ask him, "Will that work? Do I look like I've been thoroughly kissed?"

He leans down and whispers into my ear, "Bella,

with that look in your eye, you look like you've been thoroughly fucked, and it's putting all kinds of thoughts in my head."

He releases me and steps back, straightening his tie and smoothing out his jacket. "I won't be gone long."

I put my hand to my mouth and walk back into G's room. She's looking at me with a big smile on her face, but thankfully, she doesn't say anything about the way I look right now. If I look anything like I feel, there's no hiding what we've been doing.

CHAPTER 16

Lucas

I drive through downtown Whiskey Run full of frustration. I got to the office this morning, and the things that came up were definitely things that I could have handled from home. But of course, once I was in the office, there was a long list of things that I needed to take care of. My few hours at the office turned into a whole day, and after a quick look at my watch, I realize that I'm late for dinner.

As soon as I pull into the driveway, I slam my car into park instead of waiting for the garage door to open. I leave my briefcase on the front seat and run inside the house, heading straight for the dining room. When I walk in, Bella has her head down, looking at her plate, and my grandmother is giving me the evil eye.

"I'm so sorry. The time got away from me, and it was one thing after another. Anyway, I'm sorry I'm so late." I lean over and kiss the top of Bella's head, and right now with Granny glaring at me the way she is, I know it's not safe for me to go and greet her. Instead I sit down at the head of the table while putting some food on my plate.

Bella has still yet to look at me, and I know I fucked up.

Granny is not helping. "I raised you better than this, Lucas. You've been married less than twenty-four hours. It's Sunday, even. It's not even a workday."

Finally, Bella looks at me, but seeing the disappointment on her face makes me want to kick myself. She's trying to hide it, though. "Granny, I told you that I knew he was a workaholic when I said yes to marrying him. I understand he needs to work. I'm honestly not worried about it."

She puts up a good front, but I can hear the break in her voice. I fucked up, and she's trying to defend me. I look at the two women and then focus on Bella. I grab her hand. "I'm sorry, Bella. I promise to do better. Do you think you'd like to go dancing after dinner?"

She answers immediately. "Sure, that sounds fun."

I sit through dinner with my granny glaring at me. I'm sure that the chicken cordon bleu is cooked to perfection, but I barely taste it as I try to figure out what I need to do to get back in not only my granny's good graces, but also Bella's. I keep one hand on Bella's while I eat with the other. As soon as we're all finished, Betsy comes to help my grandmother upstairs. She points at both of us. "Have a good night, you two."

We nod, and as soon as she's out of the room, Bella says, "You don't have to take me dancing."

I know she's giving me an out, but I don't want one. "We have to. You know Granny will know if we didn't."

She nods. "Right. Okay. I may see if Carlotta and Dwayne want to meet us there, okay?"

I nod. A buffer is not a bad idea. I already know that dancing with her is going to be torture. "Sounds like a good idea. I'm going to clear the table and change clothes. Meet down here in thirty minutes?"

She walks out of the dining room, and I rush around to get the table cleared, shower in the hallway bathroom, and Bella and I come down the steps together. We're both quiet as I drive us to the Whiskey Whistler. I try to fill the silence with small talk, but all I get from her are one- and two-word answers. When we finally get to the bar, Carlotta and Dwayne are already there. We no sooner get to the table than Carlotta whisks her away, leaving Dwayne and me staring after them.

"So how's married life?" he asks me.

I try to see if he knows our situation, and he doesn't leave me hanging. "I know, but don't worry. Carlotta swore me to secrecy, and I promise you, there's no way I'm getting on her bad side."

I laugh at that. "It's good. I've already fucked up, though."

He waves at the waitress, and she stops at our table. "What are you having?"

I shake my head. "Nothing for me. I'm driving. I'll get my wife a beer, though. Whatever you have on draft."

The waitress takes Dwayne's order, and when she walks away, I find my wife on the dance floor. Dwayne clears his throat. "So you already fucked up, huh? You do realize you've just been married twenty-four hours, right?"

I laugh, and the waitress comes back. She sets the beers on the table, and I turn to Dwayne. "Yep, trust me, I know. Obviously, I'm not going to be any good at this and poor Bella. She definitely got the raw end of the deal."

Dwayne takes a drink. "Okay, I'll bite. What did you do?"

I steady a look at him to read his reaction. Maybe then I'll know exactly how bad I fucked up. He's been married awhile, so I'm sure he can give me some advice. "Okay, uh, I went to work for a few hours today. My assistant said some things came up. I ended up staying all day and was late for dinner."

His forehead creases. "But it's Sunday."

"Fuck man, I know. Kelly said there was something up with one of the accounts."

"Oh fuck," Dwayne says. "Kelly's your assistant, right? Fuck, I've heard all about her."

I shake my head, not understanding. "What do you mean, you've heard all about her?"

"Uhhhh," he stutters and holds his hands up. "Forget it. Forget I even said anything."

I would laugh at the scared look on his face if I wasn't seriously trying to figure out what's going on here. "No, really, what is it?"

He shakes his head, and I lean toward him. "Look, Dwayne. There has to be some kind of bro code or something here, right? If you can help me out, that would be great, especially seeing as how I'm so new to this and obviously have no fuckin' clue what I'm doing."

He laughs at that and looks at his wife on the

dance floor. Bella and Carlotta are barely moving and seem to be in a big discussion about something.

Dwayne blows out a breath. "Fine, but don't use this against Bella because if you do, I'm pretty sure my wife will put me in the doghouse–literally the doghouse–for a week. She loves her friend, and I don't want to betray my wife or Bella."

Now I'm more curious than ever. "Fine. I promise. Now what about Kelly?"

He shrugs. "I've just heard the girls complaining about her, that's all. She's not nice to Issi at all. I guess Kelly has some kind of hold on you... she's been after you for a while. I'm sure that's probably why Bella took today so hard. I mean besides the fact you went to work on a Sunday the day after you got married. I mean, that's pretty fucked up."

I groan and shake my head. Damn, to hear him put it that way, it sounds really bad. But I still need to clear this all up. "There's nothing between Kelly and me. She's my employee. She's been my assistant for years, and there's never been anything between us."

He shrugs, and I look out at the dance floor. The DJ is playing a fast song, and there's a man that has come up to talk to Carlotta and Bella. It's obvious by the way he's talking to my wife that he's making a move on her, and I don't like it one bit. I stand and watch, and it's the hardest thing I've ever done. He hasn't touched her, but the way he's leaning over to talk into her ear has me seeing red. I can feel Dwayne's eyes boring into me, and it's not like me to cause a scene, but I can feel the rage building inside me. The DJ announces that he's switching it up, and a slow song comes on. I'm off the stool and across the bar in an instant. When I reach Bella, I don't give her a choice. I pull her into my arms and away from the man that I'm pretty sure was going to ask her to dance with him.

"Uh, hey," she says, looking up at me.

I try to calm myself, but it's impossible. Through gritted teeth, I ask her, "Did you forget you were married, Mrs. Blaze?"

She scrunches up her nose. "What? Of course not."

"I would appreciate it if you didn't grind on other men."

She stops dancing. She's mad. I've never seen her look so mad. "I wasn't grinding–"

I interrupt her. I'm angry too, and I don't know how to deal with it. I've never been the jealous type, but tonight I'm filled with it. "You're mine, Bella." I catch myself because I know I'm saying too much. "I mean, as long as we're married, you're mine."

She puts one hand on her shapely hip. "I know that, Lucas. It's not me you have to worry about cheating." She lifts her hand up and pokes me in the chest with her finger. "Maybe instead of pointing fingers, you should look in the mirror."

I grab her hand and hold it against my chest. "Me! Let me explain something to you. I don't cheat."

She laughs, literally laughs in my face. "Right."

She wants to say more, but she doesn't, and I lean down to look in her eyes. There's a mixture of every emotion in there, and I don't know what the hell to do with it. "No, tell me what you meant by that statement *look in the mirror*. You think I've cheated on you?"

She looks around the room, and we are getting stares from people. I see that Dwayne has made his way to the dance floor, and he and Carlotta are dancing. Carlotta is giving me dirty looks, so I can only image what Bella's told her.

Bella looks up at me. "Either start dancing or walk me off the dance floor, Lucas. If you don't, we'll be the talk of the night, and your grandmother will hear about it by morning."

Fuck! That's one negative about being a Blaze and living in a small town. Everyone's in your business. I start to sway back and forth and tuck her against my chest. I may be dancing, but this isn't over. I lean down and whisper to her, "Bella, honey, I know I fucked up. I really thought there was a problem with an account today. But when I got to the office, there were all kinds of things that needed done. You know how I am when it comes to work."

She nods and finally lifts her eyes. "Right. Honestly, it's none of my business, Lucas. All I'm saying is that if you're going to... ya know, you may want to be more discreet is all. I mean, going to work on a Sunday with your assistant the day after you get married... I'm just saying it's not a good look for you. For me. For us. I mean, I know this marriage is a farce, but-"

I bring my hands up to each side of her face and tilt her head. When her eyes are locked on mine, I tell her, "I don't cheat, and I sure as hell wouldn't cheat on you." I can see the hurt in her eyes. "Talk to me... there's more."

She juts her chin at me. "Every boyfriend I've had has cheated on me, Lucas. I just don't want you to. I know I have no control over what you do, and it's stupid of me to even feel this way."

When I proposed marriage to her, I wasn't ready for all these emotions that I'm feeling and I don't know what to do with. But this right here, I can take care of her insecurity. "Well, they're dumbasses, Bella. I wouldn't do that to you. I haven't even looked at another woman since we decided to do this." I blow out a breath, and my body trembles. "Honestly, I wasn't prepared to be jealous and feel like I need to claim you right in the middle of a bar."

She stutters over the words. "Claim me?"

I nod as I run my thumb over her lip. "Yeah, honey, claim you. Let all these men know you're mine."

I can't take it anymore, all this back and forth. I can still feel the pit in my stomach from when that man was flirting with her, and the only way I know how to deal with it is to make sure every motherfucker in here knows she's mine. I press my lips onto hers and savor the feel of her against me. I think the music has changed, and I can feel people jostling around us, but I don't let Bella go. I kiss her thoroughly, wanting her to not have any doubt that there's no way I'll be cheating on her. She pushes herself flush against my body, and I know she can feel the swell of my cock against her belly. I want to touch her everywhere, but instead, I pull back and look at her swollen lips. She starts to step back, but I put my hand on her lower back to keep her right where she's at. My voice is gruff. "If you step back right now, the whole damn town is going to know exactly what I want to do to you right now."

Her eyes are glazed over, and she hasn't had the

first drink. She blows out a breath. "You mean they won't know from that kiss?"

I chuckle and lean down to kiss the tip of her nose. "Dance with me."

She nods, and I wrap my arms around her as we sway to the music. We're not on beat or any kind of tempo with the fast music that's playing, but I'm learning that we may be creating our own kind of rhythm.

Isabella

Since the night at the bar, we've been closer than ever. He's taken to working at the house in the mornings and then going to his office in the afternoon. He's made it home for dinner every night, and he's always touching me. Well, except in the bedroom. It's like in there he can't get to the opposite side of the bed far enough. But I'm not complaining. G is happier than I've seen her in a long time. We spend our evenings with her, watching television. We found that both Lucas and I love Westerns, so we've filled our nights watching those with his granny.

I just got off the phone with Carlotta and walk into the living room. Granny is seated on the couch, eyes glued to the TV. Lucas is sitting in the recliner, and his eyes find mine. His gaze travels the length of me and back up again before he holds his hand out to me. "Come and sit with me."

Granny snickers, and I know I can't deny him. I walk across the room and gingerly try to sit on his lap. His hands go to my waist, and he pulls me down until I'm fully seated. He pulls the lever of the chair, and our legs and feet rise in the air. He tucks mine between his. I'm rigid as a board, and he leans into my ear and whispers, "Relax."

I whisper hiss back at him, "I'm too heavy."

His arm snakes around my waist, and his big hand settles on my belly. "You're perfect, Bella."

With his other arm, he grabs a blanket and pulls it up over us. Between the warmth of the blanket and the heat of him surrounding me, I burrow into him. He grunts, and I tell him, "I told you."

He wickedly kisses my ear. "That's not what the groan was about."

My eyes widen, and my mind goes a mile a minute.

The movie continues, but I have no clue what's going on. All I can think about right now is Lucas.

"Well, I think I'm going to go on to bed, you two."

I hate the thought of getting up, but I start to sit up. "I'll help you, G."

She waves me off. "Nonsense. I texted Betsy, and she's on her way."

I take a minute to look at G, and her color is off. She looks really pale. "Are you feeling okay?"

She waves me off. "Yes, I'm fine."

But I can tell she's not telling me the whole truth. She's out of breath just moving to the edge of the couch. "G, don't lie to me."

She opens her mouth to do just that but then thinks twice about it. "I'm a little more tired than normal, but that's all. I just need some sleep."

She tries to give me a smile to let me know she's okay, but I see right through it. Betsy comes to help her up to her room, and I tell her to let me know if she needs my help at all tonight. Granny gets two steps and Lucas is lowering the feet of the chair. He helps me up and then sets me back down, telling me he'll be right back before going to his granny.

He lifts her up in his arms. "One ride to bed coming up."

Granny, Betsy, and I all chuckle as he carries his granny from the room.

"Good night," I call to them.

How in the world am I supposed to stay immune to Lucas when he does things like this? Seeing him with his grandmother and how he cares for her is enough to make me swoon. Heck, even the hardest of hearts would swoon watching him with her.

He comes back and heads straight for me.

"Uh, do you want me to move now?"

He lifts me up, sits down, and pulls me back into his lap. Literally in three seconds, he has us back in the same position as before. "Why would I want you to do that?"

I shrug, trying to remind myself this is all for show. The lines are all getting confused now. "Granny's not here... we don't have to... you know."

"Stay," he commands.

I lie back in his arms. His hand trails across my belly back and forth. He pulls my hair back, exposing my neck, and presses his warm lips to me there. I close my eyes as all the sensations ricochet in my body. My nipples harden almost painfully. There's a tug in my lower belly, and I'm sure that there's a wetness between my thighs just like any other time Lucas has touched me.

"Give me your mouth."

I don't hesitate. I turn my head, and he kisses me until my toes curl. He groans when he pulls away. "I want you."

I may regret this in the end, but there's no way I can deny him. "You can have me, Lucas."

He hooks his foot around my ankles and shifts my

legs open. His hand trails between my thighs and presses against my hot core. Even through the thin sleep pants and underwear, his touch is intense. It's not enough, though, and he must feel the same because he goes back to my waist and slides his hand down under my pants and panties. When his bare fingers touch me, my hips jerk, and he chuckles in my ear, "You like that, do you?"

I nod jerkily. My breaths are coming in little pants as he strokes his finger through my wet slit. I bite on to my lip to hold in the groan because I swear I've never felt anything so good in my life.

His thumb brushes across the swollen bundle of nerves, and I grab his arm and squeeze. He kisses my cheek. "Damn, Bella, you're so damn responsive."

I clench my eyes closed because I know I need to tell him. I blurt it out in a rush. "I'm a virgin... I've never done this before, Lucas."

"Fuck," he groans. "No one's ever touched you here?" he says, patting my bare pussy.

My knuckles turn white as I squeeze the arm of the chair. "No, no one."

"How? Fuck don't answer that. Their loss is my gain. Lie back, honey. Relax and I'm going to take care of everything, okay?"

I nod and lay my head back on his shoulder. "Let

go of my arm, baby. Grab the chair with both hands, okay?"

I do as he asks, and I'm lying here on top of him. I lift my hips as he pulls my pants down to my knees. The covers fall to the floor, and I'm lying wide open with both his hands between my legs. I've never in my life been this exposed, but all insecure thoughts go out the window when he moves one hand to my entrance and buries his finger knuckle deep inside me. He plunges in and out of me slowly. "That okay?"

I moan. "Yeah."

He kisses my cheek. "Not enough, though, is it?"

I shake my head. "I'm not going to have you tonight, Bella. You deserve more than to be fucked in a chair like this, but I am going to make you feel good."

I moan, and he leans forward, pressing his lips to mine, swallowing my moan. He kisses me thoroughly before pulling back. "You have to keep it down, okay, baby?"

I nod.

As he finger-fucks me, his other hand moves to my clit. He's circling it, slow and steady and then fast and hard. He doesn't stop, and I start to squirm in his lap. He's bringing me to the edge and then he lets off, over and over, until I'm pleading with him to give me a release. "Please, Lucas. Please."

"You need to come, Bella?"

I grunt as I gyrate my hips and ride his hand. He's relentless as the orgasm shoots through every nerve ending of my body. My whole body arches, but he doesn't let me go far. I ride out the pleasure, thrusting my hips against his hands. Never in my life have I ever felt anything like it, and he doesn't stop. It's like he's on a mission to give me pleasure until I'm just a lump of limp arms and jellied legs.

When I fall back onto him, he chuckles. The rumble of his chest vibrates against my back. He brings his hand up, and it's covered in my slick arousal. He brings it up to his mouth, and I suck in a breath as he licks his fingers clean. He moans as he tastes me from his fingers. "Fuck, Bella, you taste good."

That right there intensifies everything even more. I try to turn in his arms. His hard bulge is evident at my back. "I want to taste you too."

He reaches for the lever and lowers our feet before pulling us both up from the seat. I reach for my pants and pull them up my thighs. He grabs on to my hand, and we walk upstairs. My heart is racing as I wonder if this is it. Will I finally lose my virginity? And with Lucas Blaze, the man I've secretly been in love with forever?

We walk across the threshold of our bedroom hand

in hand. I remind myself to breathe and let it out in a big pant. He pulls back the covers and helps into me bed, but he surprises me when he pulls the covers back up over my body. "Lucas?"

His jaw is pulled taut. "I don't trust myself with you alone right now. We can't take this to the next level because it changes everything, Bella. I'm going to go downstairs and work."

My mouth drops open. I want to argue with him and tell him that nothing will have to change, but I know I'd be lying. Even now, I feel like everything has changed. The rules of our game are no longer black and white. I close my mouth and nod.

He leans down and kisses me on the forehead. Without another glance, he walks out of the bedroom and shuts the door behind him, leaving me to my thoughts and my still recovering body.

Lucas

I pry my eyelids open and squint at the morning light coming through the curtains. I feel like I have a hangover, but I didn't have a drop to drink last night. All I can blame it on is my lack of sleep and the fact that I fought hard with myself all night. It took everything I had to walk away from Isabella, and when I did, all I could think about is saying to hell with all the rules and taking her like I want to. But I didn't.

Things are getting complicated, and I'm starting to feel things that I don't want to feel. I went downstairs and took a cold shower and then worked a few hours. I thought I'd sleep on the couch in my office, but I eventually found my way back to the bedroom and made sure to stay on my side of the bed. Even though Bella with her bare leg hanging out of the cover was tempting as fuck.

This morning, I'm painfully hard, and Bella has found her way to my side of the bed. She's sprawled over top of me, and when she shifts, I groan loudly. She wakes up, lifting her head off my chest and staring at me wide-eyed. She starts to move off me, and her leg nudges against my hard cock. I put my hands on her back to hold her still as a guttural groan comes from deep within my chest. I'm hurting, but fuck, it's a good kind of hurt.

She stops moving and stares at me. She smiles as her hand travels down my bare chest, my stomach and to my shaft. Her eyes widen when she tries to wrap her hand around me. "Wow," she says, impressed.

I try to keep my hips still even though I want to nudge them into her hand to let her stroke me. I'm concentrating hard because it wouldn't take much for me to blow a load in my shorts right now.

"Bella," I warn her.

She wraps her hand around my girth and moves it from root to tip. "Wow, is that for me?"

Just her words have me thinking about shoving her to her back and burying my cock deep inside her. But I try to keep my wits about me. "We shouldn't..." I start.

Is she disappointed? For just a second, I think so, but the look disappears quickly.

She's smiling at me with rosy cheeks. "Let me take care of you, husband."

I don't know if it's what she's offering to do or her calling me husband, but it has me lifting my hips into her hand. She raises to her knees, and I reach for her, but she moves out of my grasp.

The covers are thrown to the floor, and Bella is sitting between my legs, her hands on my thighs. Her appreciative gaze goes over my bare chest and abdomen, and she frowns at my shorts covering my lower body. Her fingers go to my waistband, and she tugs them down. I lift my hips as she pulls them down my thighs. It's awkward as she tries to get them off, but we make it work. When she sees my bare cock, I swear she licks her fuckin' lips. Precum oozes from my tip, and we both watch as it starts to roll down my thick shaft. Before I can even wrap my head around what's about to happen, Bella leans forward and pokes her little pink tongue out to catch it. She doesn't stop there. She runs her velvety flesh along my length to the tip and licks her lips when she's done.

My hand goes to the back of her neck. "You don't have to do this, Bella."

She looks at me worriedly. "Am I doing it wrong?"

I shake my head. "You couldn't do it wrong if you tried."

She smiles broadly and scoots even closer. Her hand goes around my base, and she opens her mouth to take me in.

"Aww fuck," I groan as her hot mouth wraps around me.

She starts to move, up and down. She whimpers and hums around my cock and sucks me greedily. My hips start to move on their own. "So close."

She takes me deeper, and I hit the back of her throat. Her eyes widen, but she doesn't stop. Over and over, she takes me, until I'm fucking her face. I can't take my eyes off her. "Damn, baby. I'm about to come."

She moans and nods her head.

I gently pull at her hair. "Fuck, unless you want a mouth full of cum, you'd better stop."

But she doesn't stop. If anything, she moans in approval, and it's two more strokes before my hips start to jerk violently. There's no stopping as I thrust in and out of her mouth. She takes it all, and when I'm completely spent, she pops off and swallows.

I pull her up the length of my body. She settles a knee on each side of my stomach and presses down into me.

I'm searching her face for any regret, but I don't find any. All I see is a woman that needs to be satisfied. "You okay?"

She rubs her panty-covered pussy across my belly. "Yeah," she answers in a groan.

I toss her off of me onto her back. I lift her shirt up and suck her nipple into my mouth. Her back arches off the bed as she runs her fingers through the hair at my nape. I can already feel my cock hardening, and I press my hips into the bed. It's her turn now.

I suckle her other breast before kissing down her stomach. With one hand, I help her out of her bottoms and go straight for her pussy. All I've thought about since last night is that I need another taste of her, and this time I'm taking it by mouth. She's wet and slippery as I gently push my finger inside her. I lick her sex in one big stroke. Already my chin is soaked with her juices, and I suck her clit into my mouth. She raises up, and I throw an arm over her waist to hold her down. Relentlessly, I eat her pussy, suckling her as if this is my last meal. Her hands are pulling at the bed sheets, and her hips are thrashing, but I don't stop. I need her to feel what I feel. I need her to know it's me that can make her body hum. I'm the one that she needs when she wants to get off.

She comes in an instant, her whole body stretching

taut underneath me. I lap at her as tiny tremors rock through her. It's not enough. I'm beginning to wonder if it will ever be.

I climb up her body and lie next to her, pulling her against me. She curls into me, and I lift my head to look at the clock. "I think this is the first time in years I've overslept."

She asks me tiredly, "What time is it?"

I yawn loudly. "Eight."

She lifts her head from my chest and turns to look at the clock. "Oh my God, I need to get dressed. G is probably already up."

I lie in the bed with my hands behind my head and watch her run around. She's bent over trying to find her shorts that I tossed, and I have a perfect view of her round ass. As if she's just now realizing it, she bolts up straight. "Are you looking at me?"

I lean up on my elbows. "You're naked from the waist down, wife. What else would I be looking at?"

She smiles softly at me even though she pulls her shorts on to cover herself. I turn to my side to watch her. "Don't forget the fundraiser for wounded heroes is tonight."

She raises up to look at me. "You want me to go with you to that?"

I laugh. "Yeah, of course I do."

She shakes her head. "Lucas, that's not really my thing. I mean, I won't know anybody... What if I embarrass you or say something wrong? I should just stay here."

I sit up in the bed and move to the edge. "No way, honey. First of all, you'll know me, and I won't leave your side." I almost tell her that she'll know Kelly, but from what I heard from Dwayne, it's probably not in my best interest to mention she'll be there. "Go with me, Bella. We'll have a good time."

She smirks and rolls her eyes. "You know I can't tell you no."

"You may not want to tell me that because I may use it to my advantage."

She turns to go to the bathroom before looking over her shoulder at me. "I think you already have there, husband."

She shuts the door behind her, and I fall back on the bed. I wait for the panic or feelings of overwhelm to settle in, and when it doesn't, I begin to wonder if maybe, just maybe, Bella and I could really have something here.

CHAPTER 19

Isabella

It's been a rough day.

This morning was perfect, but as soon as I made it to G's room, I knew something was off. She didn't want to admit it, but she wasn't faring well today. Her shortness of breath is getting worse, and she stayed in bed most of the day. I tried to convince her to let me take her in to the hospital to get checked out, but when she refused, I called in the doctor. She didn't want me to call Lucas and his brothers or their dad, and so I paced back and forth while the doctor checked on her.

She has swelling of her feet, fatigue, weakness... all the symptoms we knew were coming. She has end-stage heart failure, and even though we knew she didn't have long, we thought with how she's been doing lately we would have longer.

I secretly text Lucas because I don't know what else to do. He would want to know that his granny has taken a turn for the worse. *The doctor is here with Granny. She's having a rough day.*

Instead of texting me back, he calls.

I try to control my voice when I answer, but it's shaky. "Hey, Lucas."

"Hey honey, you okay?"

I grip the phone tighter. "Yeah, I'm okay. I just hate seeing her like this."

His voice is deep and thoughtful. "We knew it was coming. All we can do is try to make it easy for her."

I barely resist rolling my eyes. This is his grandma we're talking about, and he's trying to soothe me. I'm supposed to be the professional here. I strengthen my nerves and start relaying the treatment we're starting. "The doctor gave her some medication to let her rest. We've upped her oxygen a little. She's resting now."

"Good, good. I know you're doing all the right things for her, Bella. I'm going to round up the boys, and we're going to stop in and see her, okay?"

I nod and let out a sigh in relief. "Yeah, that sounds good. She'll be happy to see you guys, but we can't tire her out."

"I promise."

I hang up the phone and make it back into her bedroom as the doctor is closing up his travel case. "She needs to rest, and I told her no more dancing today."

I smile even though it's the last thing I want to do. "Right, no more dancing."

I smile at G, and she gives me a faint smile through the oxygen mask before closing her eyes. I follow the doctor to the edge of the room. "What do you think?"

He puts a hand on my shoulder. "There's not much time, Isabella. All we can do now is make her comfortable."

I know that, and even though I ask him, I know he can't give me a definite answer. "How much time, Doc?"

He shakes his head. "When the good Lord is ready to take her home, Isabella. None of us know when."

I nod and thank him for coming.

The rest of the afternoon, I sit with G. The guys all come and hang out, each of them speaking in hushed tones. They all take turns talking to G, each of them making her laugh. By late afternoon, after her meal, she seems to have perked up a bit.

She points to the white box sitting on the chair across the room.

I look at it. "Uh, I don't know what that is."

Lucas interrupts. "That's a dress for Bella. Tonight's the wounded hero fundraiser, but we can have someone else attend in our place. We're going to stay home with you."

She takes the oxygen mask off and gives Lucas a determined look. "No you're not. Now look, I know Ford has to go be with Ollie."

Ford interrupts and mentions his assistant's name. "No, Lilian is picking up Ollie. I'm going to hang here tonight."

She looks at Beau with her forehead creased. "Beau, what about Natalie?"

He shrugs. "Natalie didn't want to go tonight anyway. She's going to stop by here for a little bit."

"See, Ford, Beau, and Austin–you know he didn't have a date for tonight–can stay here with me. Plus, Betsy is here," she says, pointing to the night nurse in the corner.

Austin laughs. "I don't know if I should be offended or not at that statement."

In true G fashion, she looks at him. "Well, did you have a date?"

He shakes his head sheepishly. "Noooo. But it's only because the woman I asked turned me down."

Lucas and his brothers all start to laugh. "What?

Mr. Romeo himself got turned down? Who is this girl?"

Granny shakes her head. "Now, boys, leave your brother alone. All players settle down at some point. Look at Lucas."

She turns back to Lucas and me. "See, you and Issi should go. You need to go show off your wife and have a good time."

I can't tell by the look on Lucas' face exactly what he's thinking, but he tells his granny plainly, "I don't want to leave you."

She waves her hand for him to come over to her. I get out my phone and start taking pictures and videos of her with her grandsons. I wish Hudson was here, but I know he would be if he could.

I can't hear what she says to him, but they hug, and he holds her for a long time. When he finally releases her, he turns to me. "What do you say? Feel like dancing with me tonight?"

I look uneasily at G because honestly, I don't feel right leaving her either. I lift my shoulders in a shrug. "If that's what you think we should do."

Granny throws her hands up. "That's exactly what you should do. Now come give me a hug, go get your party dress on, and then come back in here before you all leave so we can take pictures."

I hug G extra tight. When I turn around, Lucas is standing with the white box in his hand, and he holds his other one out to me. I take it, and we walk out of the room hand in hand. As soon as we're through the doors, I pull him to a stop. "Lucas... I don't think we should go."

He cups my cheek. "I know. I don't want to go either, but I'm not going against her tonight. She wants me to go, and she feels pretty strongly about it. We'll go for an hour or two, make an appearance, and then come home."

"Fine."

We go to our bedroom, and the bed is still unmade from this morning. I know my face is at least ten shades of red when I see the bunched-up sheets reminding me of when Lucas was between my thighs.

"Bella. Earth to Bella."

I drag my eyes off the bed, and Lucas is smirking at me. "I called your name a few times. What are you thinking about?"

"Nothing. Nothing at all."

He grins knowingly and holds the white box out to me. "Open it."

I take the box from him and open it. Inside is a fitted black cocktail dress with diamond accents. I drop the box as I pull the dress out. "Lucas, this is beautiful."

He shrugs. "Not as beautiful as you."

I almost choke up, and he puts a hand at the curve of my neck. "You okay?"

"Yeah, but Lucas, you're going to have to stop being so sweet and saying things like that."

He shrugs like he doesn't understand what I mean. "Why?"

I grip on to the front of his shirt. "Because I may start to like you even more and not want this to end."

I don't wait for him to respond. I'm too scared that I'll see fear, distaste, panic, or hell, all of the above. I walk toward the closet to find shoes and a purse to match what is probably the most expensive item in my closet.

I grab tights and shoes before walking through the closet to the bathroom. I get ready, touching up the curls in my hair and putting makeup on for the first time today. When I walk out, Lucas is stunning in a black suit and tie.

"You're breathtaking, Bella."

I look down at the sweetheart neckline. "It's the dress."

He grabs me around the waist. "No, honey, it is

most definitely you. Now let's go pose for some pictures so I can take you to the ball."

He has his arm around me and doesn't let go. Not while his brothers tell me how great I look. Not when I hug his granny, and not when we pose for at least thirty pictures. It's almost as if he doesn't want to let me go.

CHAPTER 20

Lucas

By the time we arrive at the fundraiser for wounded heroes, it is in full swing. We missed dinner, and we made it just in time for me to run to the podium and present the donation check from Blaze Whiskey.

The room is full of congressman, the governor, and CEOs of big corporations, but instead of looking at any of them, I'm looking at Bella. She has her hand to her chest, right over her heart, and I don't think anyone has ever looked at me with so much pride as she is right now.

She worried the whole way here that she wouldn't fit in or she'd do something she shouldn't. As soon as I'm done with the presentation, I walk down from the podium and meet Bella. I'm about to ask her to dance when Walker and his wife Brooklyn come toward us. I'm about to say hello and introduce them to Bella when they both grab my wife up in a hug. I'm standing here off to the side with my mouth hanging open. Walker pretty much owns Whiskey Run–at least most of it. He owns multiple businesses in downtown and a number of homes and land around Whiskey Run. He also owns a huge compound at the edge of town. He's definitely a good guy to have on your side.

Finally, Walker turns to me and holds out his hand. "I hear congratulations are in order."

I nod and pull my wife back to my side. "Yes, I was going to introduce you to Bella, but it seems you already know each other."

Walker nods. "Oh yeah, she's been out at the compound a few times when I couldn't get ahold of the doctor and I needed someone sewn up."

I don't even try to hide the shock when I look at my wife. "Really?"

Brooklyn nods. "Oh yeah, Issi has saved us quite a few times." She turns to Bella. "Bo Bo is going to be so sad when he hears you got married."

Bella looks at me, her face flaming before turning back to Walker and his wife. "Yeah, uh, so how is the project coming? You need anything else from me, just let me know."

I want to ask who the hell Bo Bo is, but I force myself to keep my cool. "What project?"

Walker lifts his chin. "You know all the property next to my compound?"

I nod. His compound is on the stretch of road from Whiskey Run to Jasper. "Yeah."

"Well, I'm putting in a facility for wounded warriors. A place for them to rehabilitate. I already broke ground, and it should be up and running in a year from now." He nods his head to Bella. "She helped us make a wish list of everything we would need."

I look at my wife in amazement. "You did, did you?"

She shrugs humbly. "It was nothing."

Walker laughs. "No, it wasn't nothing. I had the rehab specialist from Washington look at it, and he couldn't find one service, one machine, heck even any supplies that were lacking. You covered it all."

I clap Walker on the shoulder. "You need any investors, let me know. My brother Hudson is coming back soon too. I know he'd be willing to offer any expertise he can."

Walker nods. "That's awesome. I'll be in touch this week."

I nod and hold Bella's hand. "Great. Now, if you'll excuse us, I'm going to go dance with my wife."

We say our goodbyes, and I take her to the middle of the dance floor. It's only after she's secure in my arms that I ask her, "So let me get this straight... you were all worried about fitting in, and you're close personal friends with the most influential people in town?"

I can feel her lips curl up against my neck. "Uh... Walker and Brooklyn are good people."

I chuckle. "Yeah, they are."

I take in a deep breath and know I need to let it go, but I still blurt it out. "So who's Bo Bo?"

She leans back enough to look up at me. "He's a friend... one of Walker's mercenaries...he's kind of a flirt."

I hold my breath. "Did you go out with him?"

She shakes her head. "No."

"Good." I press her flush against my chest. I leave it at that even though what I really want to say is I want to talk to this Bo Bo and let him know she's off limits and she's mine. Probably if the opportunity ever arises, I'll do just that.

For now, I get lost in the music and the feel of Bella in my arms. I see men on the side that are wanting to talk to me, waving for me to come over when I'm done dancing, but I'm not in any rush. For the first time in my life, I begin to wonder if love that lasts could be a thing. Do women really ever stay? Would Bella stay? I've told myself since I was a little kid that I would never let myself fall in love, but I'm wondering if it's too late. Is this what love feels like? I want to spend all my time with her. Every minute of every day, I'm thinking about Bella. She surprises me at every turn. She's beautiful with a good heart. Panic starts to rise in my chest, but it's not because of fear or anything like that. No, it's because now I'm wondering if when this is all over... will she leave me?

"What's wrong?"

It's only when Bella asks that I realize I've stopped dancing and I'm standing in the middle of the dance floor like a statue.

Bella's hand slides up my chest and rests on my chin. "Lucas, what's wrong? Are you okay?"

I nod. "Yeah, but I think I'm ready to head home. You okay with that?"

She pulls from my arms. "Yeah, let me run to the bathroom, and I'll meet you back here. Is that okay?"

"I can just go with you."

She laughs. "To the ladies' room? Really, it's fine. And I saw the governor waving for your attention earlier. Go talk to him and I'll be right back."

I put my hands at her waist and hold on to her. I don't want to let her go, but I know I'm being ridiculous. "I did promise you that I would stay by your side."

She tilts her head to look at me. I'm not sure what she's thinking, but she goes to her tiptoes and presses a kiss to my lips. "It's okay. I won't make you go to the bathroom with me. I'll be right back." She kisses me again, and this time, I reluctantly let her go.

I watch her until she disappears out the doors to the hallway. I know that Bella and I need to talk, and it's probably best if we do that tonight. I want to know where she stands on all this, and I probably need to tell her how I'm feeling.

I walk over to the governor and shake hands with him. My thoughts are on Bella and on my granny and brothers at home. As someone that used to enjoy the nightlife and schmoozing with high society, tonight I just want to be home with Bella. To me, that sounds like a perfect night.

Isabella

I wash my hands and stare at my reflection in the mirror. I barely recognize myself with the pretty dress and makeup. This is definitely not my normal look and not one I'm all that comfortable with, but at least I've proven to myself that I can play the part if need be.

I dry my hands and walk out of the bathroom, straight into Lucas' assistant, Kelly. "Sorry," I mutter before trying to step around her.

She puts her arm out to stop me and then positions herself right in front of me. Kelly and I have never had a good relationship. I'm not sure why, but from the first time I met her, she's been okay around people, but any time we're alone she's been nothing but hostile.

"Did you really think you could pull it off?"

I take in a deep breath. I really don't want to get into this, and it's definitely not the place, but obviously she has something she wants to get off her chest. In my most bored voice ever, I ask her, "Pull what off, exactly?"

She sputters and rolls her eyes, agitated. With one hand on her hip and the other pointing a finger at me, she says, "He only married you to make his overbearing grandmother happy... as soon as she dies, he's going to divorce you."

I grab her hand and push it away from me. I've never wanted to hit another woman as much as I do right now. "Don't talk about Lottie. You can hate me all you want, but I love Lottie and won't let you talk about her. As for my husband..."

She smirks and laughs. "Husband... on paper anyway. You know he only married you to make his grandmother happy. He doesn't want you, you money hungry bitch. I would have married him for free. He'll pay you off the second she dies, and you'll be history."

My hands are fisted at my sides. I take three deep breaths and let them out slowly. I definitely don't want to cause a scene, and if I let myself hit her, that's exactly what I'll do. I barely recognize my own voice when I say her name. "Kelly, I'm sorry. I really am. I know you love him and have for some time. But he's married to me. He married me." I start to walk away and stop suddenly, flipping my hair as I look back at her. "And one more thing. I love his granny. and I would do anything for her. That includes whooping your ass if you ever talk about her again."

I stomp down the hallway toward the ballroom. As soon as I'm inside, I don't even look around, I just make my way to the exit. I need to cool off anyway. As I get to the front, Lucas is waiting for me. He looks at me worriedly. "Are you okay?"

I don't wait for him. I continue walking, and Lucas catches up with me when I step outside on the side-walk. "I had the valet pull the car around. It's coming right there," he says, pointing the opposite direction I'm walking in.

I stop and make my way to the curb. As soon as the car is in front of me, I open the door myself and drop into my seat, shutting the door behind me. The valet driver hasn't even gotten out yet.

When he does, Lucas gets in and turns to me. "What's wrong? What happened?"

"Kelly–"

He huffs as soon as I say his assistant's name. He turns in his seat and starts to pull out on the road. "I don't see what your hang-up with my assistant is. She's been with me for the last five years..."

I throw my hands up in frustration. Is he really defending her right now? I mean, I get that she's always super nice when he's around, and she's probably a good worker, but he doesn't even know the half of it. "Well, why didn't you marry her then? If she's so great, why didn't you ask her to be your wife?"

He tightens his hands around the steering wheel. "What are you talking about? You know why I asked you? Granny wanted me to marry YOU!"

He raises his voice, and I sit back in shock. I mean, I knew why he asked me, but he's just putting it all out there in black and white. If his granny had wanted him to marry someone else, he would have done it. He could be married to someone else right now.

Someone else could be Mrs. Lucas Blaze right now.

I was the chosen one because she chose me... not him.

I put my head in my hands and try to calm myself. I knew the reasoning behind all this, but I swear I was starting to feel that this could possibly be real. That maybe, just maybe he was starting to feel something for me. Now I know that will never be the case. He married me because his granny wanted him to. It's that simple. I will never mean more to him than some fake wife. I mean, he even told his assistant about the deal.

In my most calm voice, I tell him, "You're right, Lucas. I'm sorry. I know why you married me. I just wish that you'd told me that Kelly knew all this was fake. I would have been prepared when she called me out."

He takes his eyes off the road and looks at me. "She doesn't know."

I laugh. "Yes, she does. Trust me, she knows."

He's quiet for a minute, hands flexing around the steering wheel. "Shit. She probably saw the contract."

I turn in my seat. "I never signed a contract."

He lifts his hand and runs it through his hair. "I know. You didn't want anything, and I wasn't going to make you sign a prenup, so it was only drafted with no signatures. It's probably on my desk."

I lean forward. "Wait, so this contract says what? That I'll marry you and you'll give me money?"

He winces. "Uh, yeah."

"Lucas... how much money is on the contract?"

He looks at me wide-eyed and then turns back to the road. "A million dollars."

I gasp. "A million dollars? A million dollars! Are you insane?"

He shrugs as if that money is just a drop in the hat.

No wonder Kelly called me a money hungry bitch and damn, a million dollars. I can sort of see where she's coming from.

I put my head in my hands. "We should have known that we wouldn't be able to keep this a secret. Of course people are going to find out." I raise my head to look at him, on the verge of tears. "Lucas, I did this for you and for Granny. I didn't ask for money. I didn't ask for anything."

He nods. "I know, Bella. I know."

But I can't let it go. "Do you have any idea how this makes me look?" I wave my hand in front of my face. "I mean, I know I shouldn't care what people think, but this is Whiskey Run, Lucas. If Kelly knows, everyone is going to know. People are going to think I'm–omg–that I'm extorting money from your family. Your poor grandmother. This will kill her, Lucas."

He reaches across the console and wraps his hand around mine. "She won't find out. No one will. I'll talk to Kelly. It's going to be fine."

I pull my hand from his and turn to where I'm looking out the window. I'm feeling all kinds of things right now. Hurt, betrayed, lonely, overwhelmed, and I can't shake any of it.

"Bella, I promise, I'll fix this."

I nod. "Okay, sure, Lucas."

I hate being this way. I know he didn't mean it to happen, but it just seems like everything is falling down all around me. I should have been prepared for this instead of thinking that maybe, just maybe things could be different.

CHAPTER 22

Lucas

Fuck, I feel like shit.

I carelessly left that contract on my desk and didn't think about it again. I don't even know why I printed out the damn thing. When my attorney sent it to me for review, I just hit print like I do with anything else he sends me.

I want to reach for Bella, but she's already pulled away from me once. "I promise you, Bella. No one is going to know. Kelly won't–"

Bella starts to laugh. "Right, I'm not going to put my faith in your assistant. It doesn't matter anymore, Lucas. What's done is done. Now we just have to face the consequences. All I'm asking is to keep it out of the newspaper or the tabloids. G doesn't need to hear any of this. She'll be so disappointed in both of us."

Since I can't touch her, I fist my hand and lay it on the console between us. "I know, and I promise–"

I don't get the words out because my phone starts to ring. I see the caller ID on my screen on the dash, and it's my brother Ford.

I hit the answer button. "Hey, Ford. What's up? We're on our way home."

He's quiet for a second, and both Bella and I lean up. "Ford?"

"She's gone, Lucas. Her heart just stopped. I tried..." He stops and chokes a little before continuing. "I did CPR... so did Betsy. The ambulance just got here, and they couldn't bring her back. She's gone, Lucas."

I'm shaking my head in disbelief. "Ford, I need to see her. Where is she now?"

"We're at home. The coroner is on their way. I won't let them take her until you get here, Lucas."

I hit the disconnect button on the dash and wrap both hands around the steering wheel. Bella reaches for me, wrapping her hand around my arm. "I'm so sorry, Lucas. I'm so sorry."

I look at her, and she has tears rolling down her face. I pull to the side of the road, and we bounce as the tires hit the gravel road. Once I'm at a complete stop, I pull Bella into my arms. "I'm sorry too, honey. I know you loved her too."

We hold on to each other, both of us trying to navigate this sudden grief that is overwhelming. I try to think of everything that needs to be done, but I can't think of a damn thing. All I'm focused on is Bella, crying in my arms.

She sniffs and pulls back to look at me. She lifts her hands at the same time I do. She reaches for me, and I reach for her as we wipe each other's eyes. "Granny wouldn't want us crying."

She sniffs again. "No, she wouldn't. If only we hadn't gone..."

"No, we had to go. When Granny was talking to me earlier, she insisted that we go. She didn't want to stand in the way of true love, she said. But I know Granny; she knew what was coming, and she didn't think I could handle it. She wanted me out of the house." I stop rambling and release my tight hold on Bella. "You ready to go?"

Bella nods and goes back to her seat. She doesn't release my hand, though. "I think you're wrong, though, Lucas. She knew how strong you are. She loved you and was always so proud of you. She told anyone that would listen that you were her favorite.

Your brothers all knew it, but no one ever seemed to care. Do I think she knew this was coming? Absolutely. But you know what? I think she sent you away because she thought she was protecting you. That was her last way of saying she loved you."

I put the car into gear and look at Bella. I think about everything she just said, and I know she's right. Sending me out of the house is something she would definitely do, and for as long as I can remember, Granny has tried to protect me. She was there for me when my own mother didn't want me. She was there growing up. She went to battle for me at school when I would get into trouble. Time after time, Granny was my protector, so it makes sense that she would try to protect me to the very end. "You know, Bella, I think you're right."

She nods and looks out at the road in front of us. Neither of us speak as we drive into Whiskey Run and take the turn-off for the house. When I pull in, there's a number of cars, and the coroner is already here. But I'm not worried. I know Ford will keep his promise.

I get out of the car and meet Bella at the front. We hold hands inside and up the stairs. The door is closed to Granny's bedroom, and when I push it open, my brothers are all gathered around her bed. A hush fills the room as we walk in. Each of my brothers come to hug me. Bella releases my hand and stands off to the side, her eyes on Granny. When I've hugged each of my brothers, I pat Ford on the back. "Anyone call Huddy?"

He nods and strokes his hand through his five o'clock shadow. "Yeah, but it's going straight to voice-mail. I talked to his higher-up, and they said he's in a jungle in Southeast Asia, so they don't know if they can get word to him or not."

I nod. "Dad and Charlotte?"

Ford nods. "Yeah, Mom and Dad are coming in from their trip to Paris."

My Dad and stepmom were on a three-month trip, and I'm sorry they are having to cut it short. I make my way to Bella and put an arm around her shoulder. "We need to say bye to her, honey."

She looks up at me with tears in her eyes. "I can't, Lucas. You go ahead."

I know I shouldn't force her, but I also know that she'll regret it if she doesn't. I pull her flush against my chest and hold on to her while I soothingly rub up and down her back. I lean down to whisper into her ear, "I need you, Bella. I don't know if I can do this without you."

She nods against my chest, using my shirt to wipe her tears. She grabs on to my hand, and I walk her over to the bed. I sit down on the edge, pulling Bella into my lap, and we both look at my granny. I try to commit it all to memory. The way her hair curls on the ends and sticks up a little all over. She always complained about it. The smell of her perfume that she's worn since I was a child. The hundreds of readers glasses that she leaves around everywhere. Her hands that are frail now but at one time were strong enough to break up five fighting brothers. I just sit here and get lost in the memories.

With one arm around Bella's waist, I reach over and pull the blanket up over Granny's arms. "I love you, Granny. You were a mother to me. You loved me when others didn't. I'll never forget you, but I know we'll see each other again."

I lean over and press a kiss to her forehead and pull back and brush the hair off Bella's face. "You have anything you want to tell her, baby?"

Bella sucks in a deep breath. "I love you, G. I'll always think of you any time I dance, or when I hear rap music. You were once my grandmother's best friend and then became mine. I'm going to miss our talks. I'm going to miss you. I love you, Granny, forever."

Bella leans over and kisses Granny on her forehead,

and when she sits up, I hold her to me. "Come on, baby."

We stand up, and I nod at Ford. "Okay."

He nods in understanding and then goes to open the doors. We all stay by her side until she's loaded onto the gurney. We walk beside her all the way downstairs, outside and when they load her into the car.

Ford stops next to me. "You want me to stay tonight? I can get Lilian to stay with Ollie."

I shake my head. "No, I'll be fine."

Ford nods. Austin has his arms crossed over his chest, and Beau has his glasses off, cleaning the lenses. "I'll be back in the morning. We probably need to plan the funeral."

Bella starts to speak, stops and clears her throat, and then tries again. "G had everything planned out. She didn't want any of you to worry about it after she was gone. We worked the last two months, and everything she asked for, she put in her diary by the bed. I helped her arrange it all." She looks at me and then at my brothers. "I hope that's okay."

I lean down and kiss her forehead. "Of course that's okay. I'm sure that was really hard to do, Bella. Thank you for being there for her."

My brothers all chime in and tell her thanks. Hugs

are given, and each of them leave with the promise of being in touch tomorrow.

I turn and look at the house I practically grew up in. The house I've shared with Granny since I've become an adult. It won't be the same without her here. Nothing will.

CHAPTER 23

Isabella

For three days, Lucas and I have lived in a trance. I'm worried about him. He's put his guard up, and it seems that I'm already losing him. He's gone from not being able to keep his hands off me to moving to his office and sleeping–if he does sleep–on the couch in there.

Today is the funeral. I ride with Lucas and Austin, but only because they insisted. I can tell by the way Austin keeps looking between Lucas and me that he's trying to figure out what's going on, and all I can give him is a shrug of my shoulders.

The service is beautiful. It seems as if the whole town showed up to express their love for the woman that first made whiskey in Whiskey Run. So many people come to the podium to speak and talk about how G had helped them or their family at one time or another. She has a special place in so many hearts in this town, and it's great to be a witness to it.

Probably the highlight–if there is one–is when the pallbearers lift the casket and start to carry her out of the church with Nelly's "it's Getting Hot in Here" playing in the church. Thank goodness it was the clean version. Everyone in the crowd smiled from ear to ear. I knew it was planned, and it makes me love G even more. Of course we can depend on Granny to make us smile, even at her funeral.

It's not until later in the day, when everyone has left and it's only Lucas and me left at the house that I begin to wonder about the future. I have so many questions I want to ask Lucas, but it's not the time.

He's changing from his suit, and I'm kicking off my high-heeled shoes. He's quiet, and I just need to hear his voice now more than anything.

"Talk to me, Lucas. About anything. About nothing. Just talk to me."

He pulls his shirt off his shoulders without looking at me. "What do you want me to say, Isabella?"

I suck in a breath when he uses my full name. "I dunno. Talk to me about Granny. Work. Your brothers. You've been quiet for three days, and I'm worried about you bottling it all up."

He pulls off his pants and sits on the edge of the bed. I pull a T-shirt over my head and watch him as he tries to form words. Finally, he shrugs his shoulders. "I don't know. I just keep thinking I'd give anything to hear her voice again. Even when she was trying to teach me something." He changes his voice. "Now, Lucas, you need to be open to love and when you find it, hold on to it." He laughs bitterly. "I always blew her off and said I would. Fuck, Bella, I would promise her anything at this point."

I take a step toward him, fingering the hem of my shirt. "She knew how much you loved her, Lucas. She never doubted that."

He shakes his head, and I know he's filled with regrets. He puts his hands on his knees and pushes himself off the bed. With only his underwear on, he looks toward the door. "I'm going to the office."

I almost let him walk away. Almost.

I reach out and grab his arm. "Sleep here. Stay here. With me."

He still doesn't look at me. "It's not a good idea, Bella."

I move to stand in front of him, lifting my T-shirt over my head until I'm standing in front of him in my bra and panties. "Be with me, Lucas."

Finally he lifts his eyes to mine. There's so much

sadness, so much torment in his depths, and it breaks my heart to see him like this. He leans his forehead down to mine and inhales deeply. "You don't have to do this, baby. Not like this."

I raise my hands to his bare waist and run my hands up his chest. He trembles at my touch. "I need you, Lucas. Tonight... tomorrow... forever. However long you'll have me... just don't push me away, not tonight."

Like a lion that's been released into the wild, he pounces on me. His hands go straight to my ass, and he lifts me up into his arms. I wrap my legs around his waist and kiss him as if there's no tomorrow.

He's open-mouth kissing my neck, down my chest, and he stops with a groan. "Bella, honey, you deserve more for your first time... not like this."

I struggle to get out of his arms, and he lets me slide down the length of his body. I grab on to his chin and force him to look at me. "This is what I want, Lucas. I want you. Now if I'm not what you want, then just tell me now..."

He grunts. "You know I want you."

I reach between his legs and cup him through his thin shorts. He's hard, and his hips pump into my hand. "It feels like you do."

He nods. "I do."

That's all I need to hear. I drop to my knees on the plush carpet. His cock is hard, pointing straight out at me. I peel his underwear down his legs and drop them at his feet. He steps out of them, and I wrap my hand around his girth and stroke him once, twice, and on the third time, I take him in my mouth. I swirl my tongue along the length of him, and he throws his head back with a deep, guttural "Fuck."

Over and over I cherish him with my mouth while running my hands up and down his thighs. I reach around and cup his backside, pulling him to me. He's trying to take it easy on me, but I don't want him to. I don't know if I'll ever have this chance again, and I don't want him to hold back.

Deeper and deeper I take him. His groans are loud and fill the room, but I don't stop. Not until he pushes his hips back and lifts me up by my arms in one fell swoop. I'm licking my lips. "Why'd you stop?"

He's undoing my bra, and he lets it fall to the floor as he cups each of my breasts as if he's feeling the weight of them. His thumbs brush across my hard nipples, and I arch my back, pressing myself into his palm.

I put my hands on his shoulders to hold myself upright. "Why, Lucas? Why'd you stop me?"

He reaches between my legs, rubbing the material

against my swollen, sensitive core. "I stopped because I was about to come, Bella."

He slides his finger through the leg of my panties, and his thick finger strokes through my slit. I widen my stance, grab on to his forearms, and pant, "Isn't that what's supposed to happen? I want you to come."

He grunts in frustration, and I whimper when he pulls his hand away. He rips my panties down my legs and then resumes touching me. I step out of my panties the best I can, but when he reaches forward, pressing his tongue to me, my legs give out, and I stumble backward onto the bed.

He follows me down, his knees now on the thick carpet as he licks me from my entrance to my clit. He moans loudly, and the vibrations have me lifting my hips. He pulls his mouth from me. "Fuck, you taste good. And yeah, honey, I'm going to come, but when I do, I'm going to do it right here."

He pumps his finger inside my aching sex, and I throw my head back. My whole body feels as if it's about to explode. I feel everything... and I don't want it to stop.

Lucas

She's squirming underneath me, and I hold her legs open with my shoulders. Her taste is addictive, and I could stay just like this for the rest of the night. "Lucas," she whines. "Please, I'm ready... I need to come."

"Come, baby. Come on my lips."

I flatten my tongue and lick her until her thighs are wrapped around my neck, her hand at the back of my head holding me to her while she's lifting her hips to get closer. I may die of suffocation, but what a way to go.

I slide my finger out of her and touch the puckered bud of her ass. Her pussy weeps, and I suck her engorged nub into my mouth. She spasms uncontrollably, and my balls clench as her orgasm takes over. I'm relentless, taking her to the cliff and letting her fly. Heat coils in my stomach, and I want nothing more than to bury myself balls deep inside her, but I keep licking her, prolonging her pleasure until she's limp, looking at me through hooded eyes.

I climb up from the floor and sit on the side of the bed with my back to her. She's on me in an instant, her arms wrapped around me from behind. "You're not leaving this time, Lucas. You're finishing what you started."

She kisses my back and neck. When I don't answer her, she circles me, moving to the front of me and straddling my lap.

My cock is hard between us, and I scoot farther on the bed. With my hand on her back to hold her, I look into her face. "I can't hurt you, Bella. I won't do it."

She nods. "You won't. I trust you, Lucas."

I can feel the sweat on my brow. I'm fighting hard not to come, and with her curvy body right in front of me for the taking, my body is craving a release.

I wrap my hand around my girth and squeeze. "Climb up here, Bella."

She lifts up to her knees and positions herself over me. Her nipple is right in my face, and I flick it with my tongue before suckling her. With her hands on my shoulders, she looks at me wide-eyed.

I give her a nod. "Take your time. Go slow, and you can stop whenever you want."

Her eyes are glazed over, and she lowers herself on me. I barely breach her opening, and she wraps around me like a glove. I'm holding my breath, waiting for her next move.

"You're doing so good, Bella." I lean back and look down where we're joined. "Let me in, baby. I need inside you."

She lowers herself and doesn't stop this time until she's sitting firmly with her ass in my lap and my cock buried deep in her pussy. Her nails dig into my shoulders, and her pussy has me in a vise, but damn it feels good.

"You okay?"

She nods, wide-eyed.

I kiss her. "Breathe, Bella."

She lets out a breath in a gust. She's squeezing me, and I know I need to move. I kiss her, taking her mouth, trying to divert her attention as I put my hands at her waist, lift her up, and let her slide down my length again. She groans in my mouth, and I do it again. Over and over she rides me, lifting her hips, shifting them side to side and back down again. It's the sweetest torture I've ever known.

"I need to fuck you, Bella."

She blinks at me. "Isn't that what you're doing?"

I kiss her lips and pull back. "Do you trust me?"

She gives me that smirk that I'm starting to love. "What do you think? Of course I do."

No sooner does she say it than I have her flipped over on her back. She gasps from the fast movement, but I can't stop.

I thrust into her gently, and when she smiles up at me, I have no restraint. Absolutely no willpower to control the movements of my hips.

Over and over, I plunge inside her. Big, deep thrusts until my balls are bouncing against her ass. An urge inside me ignites, and the need to possess her, to claim every whimper, every satisfied sigh, every one of her smiles is not something I can control. I'm not going to last.

I lift her hips to hit inside her at a different angle. She plants her feet on the bed and meets me thrust for thrust. I put one thumb on her swollen nub, and her body starts to twitch.

"Open your eyes, Bella. Look at me, honey."

She does as I ask, and emotion fills her face as I rock in and out of her. I can't look away from her. Knowing that I'm her first, that she's giving herself to me in the purest way possible forces an emotion to well deep inside me. There are so many unanswered questions, but right now, all that matters is she's mine. I deepen my thrusts, rattling the headboard with each shove of my hips.

Her body goes taut as her insides spasm on my cock, milking me until I shoot rope after rope of cum deep into her womb. I didn't even think about protection, and as soon as the thought hits me, I don't even try to pull out. If anything, I hold myself deep inside her until there's nothing left.

We're both panting, and when we're spent, I hover over top of her as I try to catch my breath. I start to lift off her, but she hooks her feet behind me. I lean down and kiss her insecurities away. "I'm just going to get us cleaned up. I'm not leaving."

She measures me with a look and unlocks her ankles. I slowly rise out of her, watching her face twist in discomfort. I took her too hard, too fast.

Without thinking twice, I lift her from the bed, and she squeals. "What are you doing?"

"We're going to take a shower, then we're going to sleep for a few days. What do you think?"

She stands next to me as I turn the hot water on in the shower. Her voice is soft as she asks me, "Together? We're going to sleep together?"

I kiss the top of her head. "Yeah, honey. Together."

She nods and smiles. It's good to see her smile

because I know there hasn't been a lot to smile about the last few days.

I help her into the shower and watch her as she washes herself. I try to keep my hands to myself, but already, I want to have her again. When she winces as she slides the cloth between her legs, I tell myself she's off limits. No more tonight. Surely, I can stick to that plan.

Isabella

I stretch before I even open my eyes, and a groan escapes me because there are muscles hurting that I didn't even know I had. With a satisfied smile, I curl back into the bed and sigh happily. I may be sore, but it's a good sore.

It's only when I reach across the bed and find it cold that I peel my eyes open and see that Lucas is not in the bed next to me. I lift my head, and the clock on the nightstand reads 8 a.m. I groan because we just went to sleep at five this morning. And that was after the third time that Lucas and I had sex. We were both exhausted, and there's no way he should even be able to stand up at this point.

I throw the covers off myself and look down at my

body. There are tiny bruises along my hips and arms. Red marks on my thighs and on my breasts. I smile as I remember how I got each and every mark. Already there's a pull in my lower belly because I want him again.

I climb out of bed even though my legs scream at me. I grab the nearest T-shirt that happens to be Lucas' and pull it over my head. I go to the restroom, brush my teeth, and then decide to go through the house to try and find my husband.

I don't worry about pants because Lucas gave Bridget the rest of the week off, and it's only us. I look in his office first, but he's not in there. I hear noises in the kitchen, and I walk that way with a smile on my face.

As soon as I walk through the door and see Lucas hugging his assistant Kelly, my stomach drops. They're in a long embrace and only let go once they hear me step farther into the room. "Hey," I say with my eyes trained on Lucas.

But he's not looking at me. He doesn't even lift his eyes at me once. Without him saying a word, I know he regrets last night.

"Hey," Kelly says. When she sees the hurt look on my face, she smiles even bigger.

"I have to go to Vegas. There's a company pulling Blaze Whiskey from their shelves. They're one of our biggest suppliers, and I need to go take care of it." He blurts it all out in a ramble, and I take a step toward him, but he turns to go around the other side of the island. I ignore the smug look Kelly gives me and try to get his attention. I wait for him to hug me, to kiss me goodbye... anything. But he does none of those things. Hell, he doesn't even spare me a glance.

He's walking toward the door of the kitchen, and I know I have nothing to lose. "Lucas."

He at least stops. I wait, and he finally turns around. He gives me one look, his gaze travels down my body, he winces, and then his eyes fall to the floor. "What is it, Isabella?"

I choke back the sob that is threatening to escape. "What about us? You and me, Lucas?"

He seems frustrated. "We'll talk about everything when I get back." He pauses for just a minute and then asks, "Are you... okay?"

I refuse to beg for his attention. And I'm not going to give Kelly the satisfaction and say *No, Lucas, I'm not okay. My heart is breaking in two.* So I say the only thing I can say and still save face. "Yes."

I don't wait for him to walk away from me. I walk

out the opposite entrance to the kitchen and up the back stairwell to the bedroom. It's only when I hear the front door shut that I let the tears fall. My heart literally feels like it's shattering inside my chest.

I knew the consequences. I knew it was going to end even if my heart hoped otherwise.

I cry until I can't cry anymore. Every emotion from the last few days take a hold of me, and no matter how hard I try, I can't pull myself together. Only when I'm completely exhausted, lying on the floor curled in a ball do the tears finally stop.

My eyes feel swollen, my heart is racing, and my head is pounding.

I raise up, sitting on the floor, my back to the bed, and lean my head back. I wish G was here. I clinch my eyes shut. "Oh Granny, what do I do?"

In that instant, my phone rings, and I'm ashamed that my first thought is that maybe it's Lucas. I grab it off the nightstand and see it's Carlotta, FaceTiming me.

I know I have to answer it or she'll be worried. I wipe at my face, but I know it doesn't help any. I hit the answer button and hold the phone out of view of my face. Her voice comes over the speaker. "Hel-looooo. Issi, where are you?"

"I'm here. I'm here. What's going on?"

She pauses, and I know she can hear the thickness of my voice.

Carlotta answers in a stern voice. "Isabella, show me your face."

I lower my eyes and bring the phone in front of me. She gasps as soon as she sees me, and I know it's bad, but I didn't realize how bad.

"Isabella! What's wrong? What happened? I mean, I know Granny is gone, honey, but she wouldn't want you upset. Not like this."

I nod and take deep breaths to try and collect my thought. "Uh, Lucas just left... uh he had work to do... and–"

My voice drops off, and Carlotta shakes her head. "And what? You're not making sense. What's going on?"

I take a deep breath and let it out. "I, uh... we... Lucas and I had sex."

She raises her eyebrows. "Today? Are you telling me you held out until today? I'm impressed because the way that man looks at you, he's been wanting it." She cuts off. "Wait. Did he hurt you? Is that why you're crying?"

I blow out a breath. "God, no, he didn't hurt me. Not like that. Geez, Carlotta. We had sex last night, and honestly I had to pretty much throw myself at him for it to happen. And then today. Well today, I went downstairs, and he was hugging Kelly, and then he had to go to Vegas for some kind of work thing. I think they went together. He's probably going to divorce me and marry her and… and…"–I start to cry again–"give her babies."

Carlotta looks at me in shock. "Isabella, look, with everything the last few days, you're emotional. You're obviously not thinking right. Pull yourself together. You can't work out anything until you talk to him. When is he coming back?"

I sniffle. "He didn't say."

She nods. "Okay, well first of all, you need to remind yourself that Lucas Blaze is a good man."

I nod. "I know he is." And then I think about him hugging Kelly and wince. "Most of the time, anyway."

"Right, well, this is what we're going to do…"

I know she's waiting for me to ask, so I might as well put us both out of our misery. "What are we going to do?" I deadpan.

She's walking, and I see her walk through her kitchen, living room, and then she's outside getting into her car. "Get dressed. Pack a bag. You're staying with me tonight."

"No, Dwayne–"

"Dwayne is out of town, and you and I are overdue

on some girl time. I promise that I'm not going to be annoyingly positive. I'll sit and eat a quart of ice cream and bash men all night if that's what you want."

I shake my head. "A gallon."

She holds out an arm in front of the camera. "All right, since you're twisting my arm here. A gallon. I'm going to stop and get the ice cream and then I'm picking you up. No more crying until I get there."

I nod.

She tilts her head and rolls her eyes. "Promise."

I agree because I know if I don't she'll keep me on the phone the whole time she goes to the store and the drive over. "I promise. No more crying... at least until I'm halfway through the gallon of ice cream."

"Deal. Go get ready."

I tell her to be careful and then hang up the phone.

I gather everything I need to spend the night. I change the sheets and make the bed before taking my bag downstairs. I'm pacing the entryway when I remember the gift that I have for Lucas that is hidden in the back of the closet.

I run back up the steps and into his room. I grab the stuffed bear, cradling it fondly in my arms before placing it against the pillows of the made bed. It may have been a crazy thought, but I think it's something he would want regardless of what happens between us now. The gift looks almost childish on the king size bed with designer blankets and pillows, but I remind myself that it's the thought that counts. And even if I'm mad and hurt right now... I still want him to have this.

CHAPTER 26

Lucas

I *shouldn't have left the way I did.*

That's what I keep telling myself the whole way to the airport. I'm sitting in the back of the Town Car with Kelly. The plan was for her to fill me in on everything I need to know for this trip on the way to the air strip, but so far, I haven't been able to focus. I'm too eaten up with guilt.

I close my eyes, and images of Isabella fill my head. Flashes from last night when I was too rough with her. I saw the bruises on her body this morning when I woke up. I was physically ill knowing that I'd put those marks on her. She has to hate me. Fuck, I know I do.

The look she gave me in the kitchen this morning, I wanted to say more, and then I saw the bruising on her thighs glaring back at me. I don't deserve her.

"Lucas... are you even listening to me?"

I shake my head, trying to force thoughts of Bella away, but I know it's worthless. "Yes, I'm listening."

She leans over and puts her hand on my knee. "Look, it's been a rough few days for you. I think it's best if I just go with you. We can do the meeting and then maybe sightsee while we're there."

I frown down at her hand on me. I have the same pit in my stomach that I had when she hugged me at the house today. She was only trying to show her condolences—or at least I thought she was—but as her hand rubs my knee, I'm wondering if that is the case. I lift her hand by the wrist and remove it from my leg. I turn to her but scoot back to put more distance between us. "So tell me again, what's the issue with the Vegas stores?"

She shrugs, and her eyes shift. "Jim is getting antsy. I'm sure he's worried about how everything is going to play out since your dear grandmother passed away."

I frown. "Uh, Jim's never met Granny. He came on after my brothers and I took over from our dad. I'm surprised he'd be threatening to pull..."

She lifts her hand to reach for me, but I tilt my head and glare. She puts her hand back in her lap. "I'm sure once we get there, we can smooth things over. It will all work out."

I pull my phone from my pocket. I search through my contacts and find Jim Baker and call him. I put the phone on speaker, and the look on Kelly's face gives me all the explanation I need. Her eyes are round in shock, and her mouth is hanging open.

Jim answers on the first ring. "Lucas, I didn't expect to hear from you. I'd heard about Lottie. On behalf of my family, let me offer our prayers and condolences."

"Thank you, Jim, I appreciate that. I was hoping to talk to you about your Vegas stores. Do you have a minute?"

Jim cuts me off. "Now, Lucas. I know you don't want to be working right now. You need to take a few days off, son. You need to process everything. We had a late shipment, but I told Kelly we found out it was because a truck broke down. We were able to go get the product, and everything worked out. I don't want you to worry about a thing."

We're pulling up to the airstrip, and I frown at Kelly. "So everything else is good? No problems?"

He laughs. "You know me, Lucas. If there was one, I'd shoot you straight with it. We're good, and I look forward to seeing you next month. You still coming out west then?"

I try to soften my voice to hide the anger I'm feeling. "Yes, I'm looking forward to it. Thanks, Jim. Tell Peggy I said hi."

"Sure thing, Lucas. See ya!"

I hit the disconnect on the phone and glare at Kelly. "What were you thinking?"

She lifts her hands. "I thought you needed a break. I was trying to help you."

I shake my head and spit the words at her. "I left my grieving wife, Kelly."

I'm so stupid. When Kelly texted early this morning, I let the chaos happen. Fuck, I welcomed it. I had just seen what I had done to Isabella, and I wanted to escape. Now all I can do is try to figure out how to make this right.

Kelly looks at the airplane on the concourse that is waiting for us to board. "Look, we're already here. The jet is here. There's no reason why we can't–"

I cut her off. "Are you even listening to me? I left my grieving wife. Bella is home..."

"She's not your wife... I know it's all fake. Your granny is gone, and it's over. She'll take her money–"

I hold up both my hands. "Stop. Stop talking right now. For the next sixty seconds, you're going to shut up, and I'm going to talk. My marriage is real. We are married, the license is filed. Bella did not take any money. Not a penny. And right now, I'm going to go home and plead and beg for her to forgive me." I take a deep breath. "Now as for you. You are going to get out of my car. You are fired. You can pick up your things tomorrow morning. And so help me, if I hear any talk from anyone in town that my marriage is fake, you will be sued for violating the NDA you signed. Do you understand me?"

"Lucas, I–"

"There's nothing I want to hear from you except *Yes, I understand, Mr. Blaze.*"

She grabs up her briefcase and opens the door. In the most timid voice I've ever heard from her, she repeats what I said. "I understand, Mr. Blaze."

She steps out of the car, and I lean up to the front seat. "Take me home, Mark."

"Yes, sir."

The whole way home, I think about what I'm going to say to Isabella. How I'm going to apologize and beg for her forgiveness. She was right about Kelly, and I didn't see it. I completely fucked up everything this morning by running out the way I did. Fuck, she probably doesn't even want anything to do with me after the way I manhandled her last night.

We finally get home, and I'm out of the car in a sprint. I unlock the front door and run inside. I don't see her anywhere downstairs, and so I run up the steps. "Bella!"

I go straight to our bedroom, and the first thing I notice is the made bed. My stomach drops. Did she leave me? *God, no, please tell me she didn't leave me.* I go to the closet, and her clothes are still there. I go to the bathroom and most of her stuff is there, but her toothbrush is gone.

It's not until I go back to the closet that I notice one of her duffle bags is gone. "Fuck!" I scream into the empty house.

I go to the bed and sit down. Pulling out my phone, I call Bella, holding my breath while it rings. When her voicemail picks up, I hang up. Fuck. I don't know where she's gone, when she's coming home. I know absolutely fucking nothing.

I pick up the bear on the bed and hold it in my lap. It's a little gray bear with round glasses. I've never seen the bear before, but it has to be Bella's. I am about to toss it on the bed when it makes a sound, and I tense in shock. That sounds like... no it couldn't be.

I hold the bear in both hands, turning it around and inspecting it. It's then I see the words *press me* on the paw. Sweat beads on my forehead, and I push the button on the bear. My granny's voice fills the room.

"Lucas, you have to be open to love. And when you find it, you have to hold on to it."

I press it again.

And again.

My eyes are filled with tears, but I press it again.

Granny knew. She knew what could come of Bella and me. She saw it even though I was too stubborn to see it myself. Fuck this bear, this recording is just another way that Bella has shown me that she loves me.

Hope rises in my chest, and I set the bear on the nightstand. I sniff and try to get my composure as I call my big brother. "Ford, I need your help."

Isabella

I lie back on the couch with my arm over my eyes. My head is throbbing from all the crying, and the light from the kitchen is not helping.

"Carlottaaaaa!"

She laughs from the kitchen and comes back, rubbing her flat stomach. "You know the ice cream was for you, and you didn't even eat it." She sits down on the end of the couch and pulls my feet onto her lap. "I'm going to be sick I ate so much of it."

"I need to get a job," I announce.

She slaps my leg. "There's no rush. I mean, really, Issi. You got married. Spent weeks planning a funeral for a woman you love that you buried yesterday. Give yourself a break."

I shake my head, overwhelmed. "I wonder what

he's doing in Vegas. I should have answered when he called. You should have let me."

She rolls her eyes at me, but I don't take offense. Carlotta is the queen of eye rolling. "It's not going to hurt him to think about what he did. Let him wonder what you're doing. You've played easy to get–"

"Hey!" I say, somewhat offended. "I'm not easy."

She shrugs. "I know that. I meant... You know what I meant. It's all right–"

But she doesn't get to finish because my phone rings again. Carlotta grabs it out of her pocket–yes, she had to hold it to stop me from calling Lucas back–and her eyes widen. "Oh shit. It's Ford."

I sit up and dive onto her lap. Ford doesn't call me. I mean never. And if he's calling me right now, then there must be something wrong. Everything starts to go through my head, and I answer the phone. "Yeah. Ford. Hey. Everything okay?"

He doesn't make me wait. "I need your help, Issi. There's something wrong with Lucas."

I jump off of Carlotta's lap and pace around the room in search of my shoes. "I thought he was on his way to Vegas."

"No, he's home. I hate to call you, but I'm really worried about him."

I pull my bag over my shoulder and am walking

out the door. "Of course, I'll go. I'm on my way. Is he okay?"

He hesitates. "Yeah, uh, I think he will be."

"Sure, Ford. I'm going right now."

I hang up the phone, and I'm opening Carlotta's car door and climbing in. Carlotta is hopping on one foot, trying to put her shoe on as she comes out of the house.

"What's going on, Issi? What happened?" she asks as she gets in the driver's seat and puts her seatbelt on.

I am not going to cry. I won't cry. "I don't know. Ford just said he's worried about Lucas." I slap my hand on the dashboard. "Go, Carl, let's go."

She laughs, and I don't see what's so funny. I fidget and bounce my leg the whole way across town. Carlotta tries to calm me, but that's not going to happen. The only way I'm going to have any semblance of calm is when I see Lucas and know he's all right. When she finally gets onto Lucas' road, I have one hand around my bag and the other on the door handle. Carlotta reaches across me, her arm over my chest. "Geez, Issi, at least wait until I get to a complete stop."

As soon as she pulls in the driveway, I'm out the door. I hear her call after me, "Call me later."

I wave a hand at her as I run into the house. "Lucas!"

I look in his office, and he's not there. I take the stairs two at a time and stop when I get to his bedroom door. "Lucas," I say, panting. "What's wrong? Are you okay?"

He's lying on the bed. He has his jeans on and a T-shirt that stretches across his chest as he leans up on his elbows. "You came?"

He looks surprised as I approach the bed. "Of course I came. Ford said he was worried about you."

I stop next to the bed and grab his wrist, while looking at my watch and counting his pulse.

"I'm hurting, Bella."

His pulse is a little elevated to be lying down, but nothing worrisome. I hold my hand to his forehead to see if he has a temperature. "Where? Where are you hurting?"

He doesn't feel warm.

Lucas lifts his hand and holds it over his heart. "Right here."

His heart. Fuck. "What kind of pain? Any shortness of breath?"

I walk away to get my bag with my stethoscope, and he grabs my hand. "No. No shortness of breath."

I look down where he's holding my wrist. "When did it start, Lucas?"

"It started when I woke up this morning and saw the marks on your body. The bruises that I put there. The pain became unbearable when I got home and you had left me."

My mouth falls open, and I look at him with surprise in my eyes. "I didn't leave you, Lucas."

He sits up on the edge of the bed and grabs my other hand so he's holding them both. "It would kill me if you did, but I couldn't.... I wouldn't blame you. The way I treated you... I knew you were sore... I knew we should have waited."

Yeah, I feel pain. But it's not the kind he's thinking. "I think we remember it differently. I had to beg you to take me, Lucas. And really, you think I didn't want what you did to me last night? I wanted it... Heck, you tried to tell me no, and I begged you for it." I jerk my hands from his and lift the T-shirt I have on. I lift up my bra and point at the marks on my breast. "These? You're sorry for these?" I let my shirt fall and then lift my shorts and point at the bruising on my thighs. "And these? Do you regret giving me these?"

His face is filled with pain and remorse, but he reaches for me. "Bella–"

I shake my head and back away. "No, I wanted everything you gave me last night. I wanted the pain, the orgasms, the satisfaction... the love. I wanted it all. I don't regret a single thing. Want to know what hurt me, Lucas? It was waking up and finding you gone from the bed. It was walking downstairs and seeing you in that woman's arms. It was..." I choke up and point at myself. "It was when you wouldn't even look at me... like I was a one-night stand that you regretted and you wanted to forget. That, Lucas. That's what hurt me."

Fuck me, I screwed up and I did it in the worst way.

I want to touch her. I want to have this conversation with her in my lap and holding on to her, but she won't let me. "I didn't regret making love to you, Bella. I freaked out this morning. I should have talked to you. Kelly–"

She cuts me off and glares. "Don't even say her name, Lucas."

I nod. "Okay, I was a fool. I really thought that our biggest client was pulling out, and yes, I was wanting to escape because I thought I'd hurt you and I couldn't look at you because I thought I'd scared you and I was afraid you would never forgive me. I was wrong. I shouldn't have left. You were right about her."

Bella crosses her arms over her chest, and jealousy flares in her eyes. "What? That she wants you? That she wants to get in your pants?"

I shrug. "No one is getting into my pants except for my wife."

She gives a gruff laugh. "Wife! For how long? Forget it, don't answer that. It's probably better if we end this now, Lucas."

"Bullshit. We're not ending a thing."

She looks so sad. Her eyes are swollen, her lips are puffy, and her nose is red. "I love you, Lucas. I have for a long time."

All of a sudden, I feel that a weight has been lifted from my shoulders, and I let out a breath. "I know that, Bella. You wouldn't have given yourself to me if you didn't."

Before she can react, I reach out and I pull her to me. I wrap my arms around her waist and put my head against her belly. For the longest time, she stands there, holding herself rigid in my arms. But I don't let go. I take deep breaths, living in the moment of having her in my arms when only minutes ago, I thought I never would again.

She runs her hand through my hair, and just that one touch gives me a little hope. But her words are like a kick in the gut. "Knowing how I feel, you have to understand why I need to leave."

My voice is thick with emotion, and I tighten my hold on her. "I need you to stay."

"Why?"

I raise to my feet and put my hands on each side of her face. The pain in her face, what I made her feel, I'll have to live with the rest of my life, but if she'll let me, I'll do everything to make it up to her. "You can't leave because I love you. Because I don't want to know what life is like without you. Because I can't let you go."

Her breath hitches, and she shakes her head as if what I just said was a lie. "You love me?"

I kiss her, molding my lips to hers. When I pull back, I don't go far. "Yes, I love you. Fuck, I love you so much, Bella. But I'm scared too. I can't lose you. If I fuck up, and I'm going to, you can't leave me."

Her hands go to my waist. "But Lucas, I didn't leave you. I was coming back. I will always come back. I promised your granny, and now I'm promising you."

My heart swells in my chest. I'm about to lean down to kiss her again when she stops me. "But are you sure? You married me because G wanted you to. Are you staying with me because—"

I stroke my hands down her back and bring her flush against my chest. "I'm staying with you because my granny was right. She told me, time and time again, that I need to be open to love, and when I found it, I needed to hold on to it."

She looks at the bear on the nightstand. "You heard it!"

I nod and lean my forehead against hers. "I heard it. That's the best gift I've ever received, Bella."

She sniffs and nods her head.

"And G's right. I've found you now, and I'm never letting you go."

I kiss her with everything inside me. I never thought I'd let myself fall in love, but with Bella, how could I not?

I pull back, cupping her face in my hands. "You know I love you. Right?"

Her hands are at my waist, and there's a challenge on her face. "Prove it."

She could ask me for anything at this point, and I'd give it to her. "Anything."

She reaches for the button of my jeans and flicks them open. I grab her hands to stop her. "Bella."

She smiles at me. "Love me, Lucas. Make me feel good."

I lean my forehead against hers. "Baby.... I can't resist you."

She pushes my hands away and pushes my jeans to

my thighs. Her hand dips into my shorts, and she wraps it around me. "Good to know."

I lift her into my arms and turn around to lay her on the bed. I lean in and kiss her neck and whisper in her ear, "Lie back, Bella. Let me love you."

Epilogue

ISABELLA

Three Months Later

I walk into the office of Blaze Whiskey with a smile on my face. I'm trying to tone it down a little and not be so obvious, but I know I'm failing.

I stop at the desk outside my husband's office, practically bouncing on my feet. "Hey, Lilian! How's it going?"

The other woman sighs in frustration, and it catches me off guard. I've never, not once, seen Lilian not completely in control of the situation. "What's wrong? Is Lucas working you too hard? I know he's trying to find a replacement for you know who."

Yeah, I still refuse to say that woman's name.

Lilian shakes her head. "No, Lucas is fine. It's Ford that is driving me crazy. I'm thinking about seeing if I can just move over to work for Lucas and let Ford find himself a new assistant."

She's not joking. I wait for her to laugh, but she doesn't. I'm about to reassure her when Ford sticks his head out his office door. "I heard that, Lilian, and you can forget that happening. You're mine."

My eyes almost pop out of my head because I've never seen this side of Ford before. He's Mr. Calm, Cool, and Collected. Not a man that barks ownership in the office.

Lilian doesn't seem fazed that Ford heard her confession or at his raised voice. She just rolls her eyes. "Sure, 'cause you're the boss of me..."

Ford stands to his full height. "I am your boss."

My head volleys between them as they go back and forth. There's definitely a sizzle in the air between them that I've never noticed before. "Lilian, can I see you in my office please?"

Lilian acts as if she doesn't hear him, and he says it again. "Lilian. In my office... please."

She huffs a breath, puts her hands on the desk, and pushes herself up. "Sure, BOSS. I'll be right there."

Lilian looks at me. "You here to see Lucas? He's on a phone call, but you know he's told me to never make you wait. You can go on in."

"Thanks," I tell her, still in shock over what's happening with her and Ford.

Ford holds the door open for Lilian, and when she passes by him, he grits his teeth and shuts the door behind him. I swear I hear what sounds like the door locking.

I stare at the door open-mouthed before finally getting myself together and walking into my husband's office. He's just hanging up the phone as I walk in. Without even saying hi, I point my thumb to the outer office. "Uh, what's going on with Ford and Lilian?"

His forehead creases like he doesn't have a clue what I'm talking about. "Beats me. What happened?"

Surely he's noticed something, but as soon as the thought comes, I shake my head. Nope, he hasn't. If he did, he would have told me.

I'm about to tell him the good news when he comes around his desk and grabs my hands, pulling me to the couch in his office. He sits down first, and I go to sit next to him, but he pulls me into his lap instead. "I have an idea."

Looping my arms around his neck, I kiss him. He

groans and pulls back. "Office sex. That's definitely an idea, but not the one I wanted to talk to you about."

"Okay, what's your idea?"

"We should get married."

I wait for him to continue, and when he doesn't, I start to freak out just a little. "Are we not married? I thought that was all official. Are you telling me that was a fake wedding, Lucas Blaze?"

He shakes his head. "No, fuck no. We're married. I'm talking about doing it again. You should get the wedding of your dreams instead of me rushing you into something. You can plan it all exactly how you want it."

I put my hands on his shoulders. "First of all, our wedding was perfect. I wouldn't have changed a thing."

He shakes his head like he's going to argue, and I kiss him. His hand comes to my breast, and he squeezes. I pull back with a laugh. "Seriously, I don't want a different wedding. Granny was at ours, and I wouldn't want to do it again without her... I mean, I want to keep that memory intact, Lucas."

He's staring at me, and I'm beginning to wonder if I upset him. "I mean, if you really want to–"

With a somber expression on his face, he looks

deeply into my eyes. "I am a lucky man, Mrs. Blaze. You continue to amaze me every day."

I shrug my shoulders with a smirk. "It's a gift. Plus, I'm not going to have time to plan a wedding."

He pushes my hair off my face and holds it in his hand at my neck. "Oh yeah, you have big plans? Something I don't know about?"

I bite my lip because it's killing me. "Maybe," I singsong to him.

When he realizes I'm serious, he sits up a little straighter. "What is it, Bella? What are you keeping from me?"

I grab on to his hand and put it to my belly. I'm holding my breath, waiting until he realizes what I'm telling him.

He stares at his hand at my midsection, and suddenly he gets it. His hand flexes protectively over me. "Are you... Are we–?"

With tears starting to roll down my face, I nod my head. "We're pregnant. Please tell me you're happy about this. I mean, you have to be, there's no going back now. And you had to know it was going to happen; we haven't used anything. But yeah... I'm pregnant. We're pregnant. You're going to be a dad."

His mouth is hanging open, and I know I've shocked him.

Seconds go by, and I lean my head toward him. "Lucas? Seriously... tell me this is–"

He cuts me off. "Perfect. Amazing. Everything. This is everything, Bella. Yes, I'm so happy. So fuckin' happy."

He holds on to me, squeezing me against his chest. I rest my head on his shoulder and sink into his embrace. "I love you, Lucas."

His voice is thick with emotion. "I love you too, baby. So much."

I pull back enough to whisper in his ear, "So how about that office sex you mentioned? I mean, we really should celebrate. Don't you think?"

He grabs the hem of my shirt and pulls it off me before letting it fall to the floor. "Definitely. We definitely need to celebrate."

He stares at my belly. There's no difference in it since this morning when he saw me before work, but he's looking at it like he's never seen it before.

I tip his chin up. His face is lit up. There's no doubt he's happy about this. "Kiss me, husband."

And he does just that.

Want to read Ford and Lilian's story?
Read it in *Something Real*.

Keep reading for the first chapter of Love Again. This is the love story of Oscar Blaze - father of Lucas, Austin, Beau, Huddy and Ford.

Read Love Again for FREE.

https://BookHip.com/ZBAKNLM

Love Again

I set my briefcase down and pull at my tie. It's been a long week, and I've never been happier that it's Friday. I have no plans except to hang with my boys this weekend.

The normally noisy house is weirdly quiet as I walk into the living room. The television is off, and there's none of the typical sounds of five boys wrestling, bickering, or even playing. As a matter of fact, I don't hear anything, and I've learned through the years that's never a good sign. I'm about to bellow for the boys when my mother walks out of the kitchen. "Hey, son. They're outside. I'm letting them run off some steam so you and I can talk."

"Hey, Mom." I throw my tie on the back of the couch and follow her back into the kitchen, instantly inhaling the sweet smell of a home-cooked meal that I didn't have to prepare. "It smells good in here. You know you didn't have to cook."

She laughs. "I didn't. I had Bridget come over and fix it. She also put meals in the freezer for the rest of the weekend."

My mouth drops. "Wow. And to what do I owe this honor? I mean I can cook." I bend down and kiss my mom's cheek. "But I don't really enjoy it, so I appreciate you and Bridget doing that for me."

She stirs the sauce in the pan and then lays the spoon on the counter before pointing toward the table. "Sit."

I laugh and unbutton the top two buttons of my shirt, but I do as she asks. "Why do I feel like I'm about to get in trouble or something? Shit... I mean shoot, did the boys do something today? You know it's the end of summer break, and I know they're a little restless."

She pulls out the chair next to me and sits down with a sigh. My mom is something else. She's been my rock, and I don't know how I would have made it these last four years, let alone the twenty-nine before that. But the way she's looking at me right now, I know I'm in trouble.

"What is it? What's wrong? Did the boys do something? Did I do something?"

She reaches across the table and covers my hand with hers. She searches my eyes, and I try to read her expression, but she's not giving anything away. I'm completely on edge now. "What? What is it, Mom? You're freaking me out now."

She blows out a breath. "How long has it been since..."— she coughs a little—"... since you... you know... spent time with a woman?"

I pull my hand back, knowing that my eyes are almost bulging out of their sockets. "Um, well, um..."

She shakes her head. "Son, Penny left four years ago."

I barely resist rolling my eyes. "I know, Mom. Trust me, I

know exactly when my wife left me and our five boys. I don't need you reminding me."

She nods and looks at me with pity. I can't handle this. The looks people give me when they find out that Penny left town without a trace. I mean, I was investigated after she left because in a small town like Whiskey Run, everyone talks. And it was too hard to believe that a mom of five boys – one of them barely a day old—would just get up and leave the hospital—leave town and her kids behind. So yeah, I get the looks where people think I'm some kind of wife killer or that I'm guilty in some way. But I can handle it. What I can't handle is the pitiful looks people give me when they finally realize that my wife left me. Literally ran from me to another country to get away. I run my hand through my hair and sigh in frustration. "What's this about, Mom?"

She shakes her head and leans her arms on the table. "I can't do this anymore."

My mouth drops, and I shake my head. "Mom, I know I put a lot on you. I told you I would hire a sitter to help out. I didn't expect you to be a full-time nanny... If it's too much, I'll hire someone."

She sits up, her back ramrod straight. "You can forget that, Oscar Blaze. You just get that thought out of your head. We're not hiring some stranger to care for my grandchildren."

"Mom, this is Whiskey Run. There are no strangers. Plus, you need help. I mean, once school starts, it will help, but you'll still have Lucas at home. I will find someone to support you as much as you need. You know that."

She pats her hand on the table and gets up to pace the room. I follow her with my eyes, trying to understand what the problem is.

"I don't need help. Son, when you took over the distillery and let me take care of the boys—well, I wouldn't trade it for anything. That's not what I'm talking about when I say I can't do it anymore."

I get up and walk toward her, stopping in front of her. "Okay, then quit talking in riddles. What's the problem?"

She throws her hand up. "You're killing yourself. You act as if you have something to prove. You've made so many improvements with the company I can't even keep up anymore. You've tripled our sales since last year."

I'm definitely not getting it. I cross my arms over my chest. "And that's a problem?"

She holds her hand up in front of my face. "I'm not finished. And then when you are here at home with the boys, you're like super dad or something. You are literally killing yourself to make sure you don't miss anything. You have five boys, Oscar. Think about it. You haven't missed anything. Not one practice, big test, game, doctor appointment. Nothing!"

Fuck, I'm starting to get a headache. "Okaaaay, so I'm not getting it. What's the problem here?"

"You have to take care of you. You're killing yourself, and you need a break."

I smile at my worried mother, but she's not having it. "Oh no, forget it, you're not going to charm your way out of this one. I've packed you a bag. You have a reservation at the Four Seasons in Jasper. I want you out of the house and don't come back until Sunday afternoon."

I'm already shaking my head. "The boys..."

She lifts her chin. "I'm staying here for the weekend, and I have all kinds of fun things planned for them. The boys will be fine."

I put my hands on my hips. "They start school on Monday."

She walks out of the kitchen, and when the door closes behind her, I have no choice but to follow her. "Mom, listen, the boys start school on Monday."

She stops suddenly, and I have to stop so I don't mow her over. She turns with her hand on her hip. "I know they do, Oscar and they'll be ready for it. You'll be home on Sunday afternoon. I'm not asking you to miss out on anything."

I open my mouth to argue and close it again. I know she's right. I know that I've been burning the candle on both ends. I thought I was hiding it, but I should know by now I can't get anything past my mother. "Okay, how about next weekend or the weekend after that? Once everything has settled down with the start of the school year..."

She starts walking again, and I follow after her. She stops next to the front door and pulls open the closet, pointing inside. "There's your bag. Everything you'll need for the weekend is inside."

I just stand and stare at her. She rolls her eyes at me. "Are you going to make me carry it out to the car?"

She reaches for it like she's going to, and I stop her. "Of course not, but Mother—"

"Mother! Ha! Is that how you talk to your mom?"

I grab the bag from the closet and hold it in front of me. "Of course not, Mom. I appreciate everything you do for me and the boys. I just don't know if me leaving right now—"

She's not listening. She opens the front door and walks outside. I follow her because I know my mother, and she'll get her way, one way or another. "Mom, are you listening to me?"

She opens the driver's side door of my SUV and points inside. "Yes, I'm listening, but I don't like what I'm hearing. You need a break. I've already told the boys that you're going out of town for the weekend. Relax... live it up... do whatever you need to do. You need this, Oscar. Your boys need for you to do this. You can't keep up this pace. I'm asking for one weekend. One! If you won't do it for yourself, do it for them."

I rub my hand across my stubbled chin and blow out a

breath. "Are you sure..."

She motions her hand toward the car again. "Yes, of course I'm sure, Oscar. Now get in and get out of here so I can take care of the boys."

I toss my bag into the passenger seat as I get in. "Fine, I'll go, but I'm not happy about it. The rules still apply, Mom. No candy. No sodas. No rap music."

She gasps. "There's nothing wrong with a little—"

I hold my hand up. "I have nothing against rap music, but the boys are a little too young for some of the language."

"Fine. Whatever you say. Basically you're telling me we can't have any fun. Got it. See you Sunday." And before I can get a word out, she steps back and closes the car door.

She's already halfway up the driveway and waving at me before I even get the car started.

I give her a halfhearted wave and start to back out of the driveway. A whole weekend without my boys. I don't even know what I'm going to do with myself.

Get the complete story for FREE here: https://BookHip. com/ZBAKNLM

Also by Hope Ford

Want more of Whiskey Run?

Whiskey Run

Faithful - He's the hot, say-it-like-it-is cowboy, and he won't stop until he gets the woman he wants.

Captivated - She's a beautiful woman on the run... and I'm going to be the one to keep her.

Obsessed - She's loved him since high school and now he's back.

Seduced - He's a football player that falls in love with the small town girl.

Devoted - She's a plus size model and he's a small town mechanic.

Whiskey Run: Savage Ink

Virile - He won't let her go until he puts his mark on her.

Torrid - He'll do anything to give her what she wants.

Rigid - If you love reading about emotionally wounded men and the women that help them overcome their past, then you'll love Dawson and Emily's story.

Whiskey Run: Cowboys Love Curves

Obsessed Cowboy - She's the preacher's daughter and she's

off limits.

Whiskey Run: Heroes

Ransom - He's on a mission he can't lose.

Redeem - He's in love with his sister's best friend.

Submit - She's his fake wife but he wants to make it real.

Forbid - They have a secret romance but he's about to stake his claim.

Whiskey Run: Sugar

One Night Love - Her one night stand wants more.

Rebound Love - She's falling for the rebound guy.

Second Chance Love - He is not a man to ignore... especially when he asks for a second chance.

Bad Boy Love - He's a bad boy that wants her good.

Whiskey Run: Guardians MC

Protective Biker - She needs his protection and he'll give it to her. But he's going to need her heart in exchange.

Broken Biker - There's only one woman for him...

Relentless Biker - He won't stop until he has her back.

JOIN ME!

JOIN MY NEWSLETTER

www.AuthorHopeFord.com/Subscribe

Be a Hottie!

JOIN HOPE'S HOTTIES ON FACEBOOK

www.FB.com/groups/hopeford

A place to talk about Hope Ford's books! Find out about new releases, giveaways, get exclusive content, see covers before anyone else and more!

About the Author

USA Today Bestselling Author Hope Ford writes short, steamy, sweet romances. She loves tattooed, alpha men, instant love stories, and ALWAYS happily ever afters. She has over 100 books and they are all available on Amazon.

To find me on Pinterest, Instagram, Facebook, Goodreads, and more:

www.AuthorHopeFord.com/follow-me

Want FREE BOOKS?
Go to www.authorhopeford.com/freebies

www.ingramcontent.com/pod-product-compliance
Lightning Source LLC
Chambersburg PA
CBHW021150310726

48971CB00002B/573